SHOWDOWN AT RICK'S

Because Clint had picked up his own pace to keep the five men in sight, he now had nowhere to go when the other man's eyes fell on him. There were no shadows or doorways that he could get to without diving headfirst.

But the men had shifted their eyes forward and were walking down the side of the street like a unit marching into war. Clint didn't like the looks of these men one bit. And the more he watched them, the tighter the knot in the pit of his stomach became.

His worst-case scenario was playing out; the men were obviously headed for his friend Rick's saloon. Not only that, but they seemed to be firing themselves up as though they expected blood to be spilled when they got there.

More than that, it seemed they expected to be the ones doing the spilling.

If Clint learned one thing for certain after watching them, it was that they weren't about to be distracted by anything less than an act of God . . .

THE GUNSMITH

283

RIDING THE WHIRLWIND

J. R. ROBERTS

JOVE BOOKS, NEW YORK

THE BERKLEY PUBLISHING GROUP
Published by the Penguin Group
Penguin Group (USA) Inc.
375 Hudson Street, New York, New York 10014, USA
Penguin Group (Canada), 10 Alcorn Avenue, Toronto, Ontario M4V 3B2, Canada
(a division of Pearson Penguin Canada Inc.)
Penguin Books Ltd., 80 Strand, London WC2R 0RL, England
Penguin Group Ireland, 25 St. Stephen's Green, Dublin 2, Ireland (a division of Penguin Books Ltd.)
Penguin Group (Australia), 250 Camberwell Road, Camberwell, Victoria 3124, Australia
(a division of Pearson Australia Group Pty. Ltd.)
Penguin Books India Pvt. Ltd., 11 Community Centre, Panchsheel Park, New Delhi—110 017, India
Penguin Group (NZ), Cnr. Airborne and Rosedale Roads, Albany, Auckland 1310, New Zealand
(a division of Pearson New Zealand Ltd.)
Penguin Books (South Africa) (Pty.) Ltd., 24 Sturdee Avenue, Rosebank, Johannesburg 2196,
South Africa

Penguin Books Ltd., Registered Offices: 80 Strand, London WC2R 0RL, England

This is a work of fiction. Names, characters, places, and incidents either are the product of the author's imagination or are used fictitiously, and any resemblance to actual persons, living or dead, business establishments, events, or locales is entirely coincidental.

RIDING THE WHIRLWIND

A Jove Book / published by arrangement with the author

PRINTING HISTORY
Jove edition / July 2005

Copyright © 2005 by Robert J. Randisi.

ISBN: 0-515-13967-X

JOVE®
Jove Books are published by The Berkley Publishing Group,
a division of Penguin Group (USA) Inc.,
375 Hudson Street, New York, New York 10014.
JOVE is a registered trademark of Penguin Group (USA) Inc.
The "J" design is a trademark belonging to Penguin Group (USA) Inc.

PRINTED IN THE UNITED STATES OF AMERICA

10 9 8 7 6 5 4 3 2 1

ONE

Normally, Clint enjoyed going back to Labyrinth. The West Texas town was the closest thing he had to a home since most of his life was either spent on the open trail or staying in a rented room somewhere or another across the country. All in all, Clint liked his style of life but was like anyone else in that it was always good to come home.

He had friends in Labyrinth who were always glad to see him. One such friend was Rick Hartman who owned a saloon aptly named Rick's Place. Hartman and Clint had been through plenty of rough times together as well as a lion's share of good ones. Rick was one of the few people Clint knew who he would genuinely entrust with his life.

But that wasn't the friend that Clint was most eager to see when he got back into Labyrinth.

It actually hadn't been that long since Clint had been through West Texas. It had only been less than two weeks since he'd been there. Before that, he'd spent some time in Tombstone after a particularly rough job he'd been on with the U.S. Marshals. Clint had taken a bit of time to rest up while in Tombstone, but had cut his trip short and left sooner than he had intented.

Tombstone was familiar territory for him as well, but was

1

one of those places that changed practically every time the sun broke the horizon. Between the miners, prospectors, and businessmen going through that place, Tombstone was made and broken more times than a gambler's bankroll.

Of course, the dustup caused by another of Clint's friends by the name of Wyatt Earp caused a fair amount of change as well. After that feud between the Clantons, the McLowerys and the Earps, Tombstone just wasn't the same.

It was a town divided. In fact, when Clint had been there most recently, he got the unnerving feeling that shots were still being fired in the alley just off of the OK Corral. It was impossible to live anywhere near that shoot-out without choosing a side. Not picking one faction or the other to throw in with, verbally or otherwise, made for some tense times.

Clint's face was recognized, and even though he didn't get more than a few harsh words thrown at him by some rowdy drunks, he could feel the glares coming at him as he walked down the street. His shoulders never really relaxed until he put Tombstone behind him.

As glad as he was to get out of there, he was even more glad to be heading back into Labyrinth. The train ride might not have been very eventful, but it was one of those times when Clint needed a good dose of dull to get himself back into a good frame of mind.

For a man who'd become accustomed to using the modified Colt that never left his side to defend his life, Clint savored the quiet times when they came his way. The trip back from Arizona was quiet to say the very least.

The train rumbled down its track, made its stops, and eventually let Clint off in West Texas. Although the seats on the train were a far cry from comfortable, the sleep Clint had gotten while in them was some of the best he'd had in a long time.

There was just something about being rocked by the motion of the train and hearing the constant clatter of the wheels against the tracks that put him out faster than a belly full of beer. The station was as familiar to Clint as the streets of Labyrinth themselves. When Clint stepped off the train and onto the platform, he couldn't wait to collect his things and find his way back into town.

Like an anxious child, Clint fidgeted the whole way until he was once again in sight of Rick's Place. The saloon was always the first thing to catch his eye since it was also one of the most crowded places in the immediate area at that time of day.

The sun was drooping low, and night was getting ready to claim the world, which meant it was time for folks to come out and have some fun after a hard day. Clint recognized a few faces and gave them all a quick tip of his hat before moving on. When he got to the door of Rick's Place, he only took half a step inside before catching the attention of the owner himself.

"Clint Adams!" Rick Hartman shouted from his spot behind the bar. "Just when I thought I'd run you out of town, you come slinking back through my door."

While a few of the strangers in town cast a nervous glance between Clint and Rick, most everyone in there knew that Hartman was just giving Clint a hard time. Soon, the good-natured belly laugh that came from Hartman was more than enough to bring everyone up to speed.

Clint stepped inside, but didn't have to go far before he was practically knocked over by Hartman's friendly back slapping.

"How the hell are you?" Hartman asked. "I hear it got a little rough with them marshals."

"Nothing I couldn't handle," Clint said with a shrug. "Although it's damn peculiar just how much a man can learn to handle."

"Some men more than others. How about a drink to wash away some of that trail dust?"

"Maybe later."

"That's right. You took the train into town. I don't know about you, but them cinders always get into my eyes, and the back of my throat always starts to taste like smoke when I ride them rails. Sometimes, it's like—"

Hartman was cut short by the warning look he spotted in Clint's eyes. Nodding, Hartman gave Clint a nudge and said, "But you don't want to hear about the tastes in my throat do you?"

"Not really."

"I knew you'd be eager to see him, and to be honest, I didn't even think you'd stop by here first."

"Actually, I thought I'd stop in and see if there was anything I should know before going over to Doc Hennessey's."

Rick shook his head and led the way back out through the front door. "Nothing but good news. The doc'll want to see you, but Eclipse will want to see you more. I swear that stallion's so anxious to run that he might kick down a wall to get out of that stable."

Only after hearing that did Clint feel back to his old self again. Covering so much ground without the Darley Arabian stallion with him had been like walking for too long without wearing his boots. That, however, was going to change real soon.

TWO

It was a short walk to Doc Hennessey's office and they got there just as the doctor was closing up for the day. The man was fresh out of his thirties and had the look about him of someone who couldn't survive more than a day or two outside of a town. He was fussing with the lock on his front door when Clint and Rick stepped up and onto either side of him.

Judging by the surprised look on Hennessey's face and the way he jumped back at the sudden sound of the footsteps coming up to him, the doctor probably thought he was being robbed. A quick look in either direction was enough to put those fears to rest, and Hennessey let out a relieved breath.

"Howdy, Doc," Rick said. "There's a visitor here to see a patient of yours."

Once his door was locked, the doctor nodded and turned to face Clint. "Yes, yes I see. I didn't think you were going to be back for a while."

"I thought I'd be gone a little longer, but I decided to head on back. Things in Tombstone aren't what they used to be."

"Um, yes. I guess that happens," Hennessey said in a

5

way that seemed more distracted than anything else. Once all three of them started walking down the street, the doctor seemed to pull himself together a bit more. He put on an easygoing smile and turned to look at Clint.

"You'll be glad to know that Eclipse is doing just fine," Hennessey said. "That wound on his leg healed up nicely. It looked like it could have been a whole lot worse. What did you say happened there?"

Clint had told the doctor when he'd dropped Eclipse off that Eclipse had been cut by a man who'd wanted to hobble the stallion to prevent Clint from chasing him down. The dirty tactic hadn't helped the outlaw one bit and had actually fueled Clint's fire to chase him down. Since the doctor no longer seemed concerned about the wound, Clint took that as good news and avoided bringing the subject up again.

"He got cut," was all Clint said. Since that seemed to be enough for Hennessey, Clint let it lay at that.

The doctor nodded. "That's right. Some horse thief or something, I believe you said. Well, not to worry. The cut was tended rather nicely at the time and wasn't much of a problem. All he really needed was some rest and a bit of care and he's ready to go. I took the liberty of putting him on a special diet. I hope you don't mind."

"Something wrong with the way I was feeding him?" Clint asked.

"No, not at all. This is just a special mix of certain grains that brought him back up to snuff. It's my own blend and it's for sale if you're interested."

"We'll see about that, Doc. For now, I'd just like to see how he's doing."

The trio had already arrived at the stable where Clint had left Eclipse. It seemed as though the Darley Arabian recognized the sound of Clint's footsteps because a very familiar whinny was coming from within the large building.

"Of course, of course," Hennessey said. "I've had him taken out for exercise every day, but it hasn't been enough to keep him from getting rather . . . umm . . . rather vocal." After another loud stomp and whinny from the stable, Hennessey shrugged and added, "I'd say he misses you."

Clint smirked and patted the doctor on the shoulder. From there, he walked straight into the stable and headed for the stall he'd rented before leaving town what seemed like months ago.

There was another man already inside the stable who'd started to approach Clint, but stopped when he got a look at his face. The liveryman seemed more relieved than anyone else and even rushed ahead to make sure the gate to Eclipse's stall was unlocked before Clint got there.

"Good to see you again, Mr. Adams," the liveryman said. "This one's been a joy and all, but he's been gettin' a might bit restless this past couple of days."

"Yeah," Clint said. "I know how he feels."

Eclipse's fretful stomping and fussing stopped the moment he got a look at who'd just walked into the stable. Immediately, the Darley Arabian's ears perked up and he pushed himself up against the gate hard enough to open it on his own.

Reaching out to lift the latch, Clint opened the gate the rest of the way and stepped inside to place one arm over the stallion's head. Eclipse lowered his head and nuzzled Clint's hand eagerly. Although the horse was still fidgeting, this time it was more of an anxiousness that came from seeing a familiar face.

"He's a strong breed," Hennessey said. "And an exceptional stallion by any means. I thought he might have needed a bit more rest, but the little bit he's gotten has been more than enough."

"Is he ready to ride?" Clint asked.

Rick let out a short laugh as he reached out to pat

Eclipse's muzzle as well. "Ready? I think there'd be a whole mess of trouble if anyone tried to stop him at this point."

"Oh, he's ready," the doctor said. "As you can see, the bandages on his leg have been replaced with a wrap and some balm."

Clint was already kneeling down to get a look at the leg that had been cut. Eclipse didn't so much as flinch when the dressings were removed. Clint flinched, however, when he got a whiff of the concoction that had been smeared over Eclipse's leg and bandages.

"It's an old mixture," Hennessey explained. "It's made with—"

"Don't bother," Clint interrupted as he stood up. "I think I recognize the smell of it. Besides, I'm sure if I want any you'll be willing to sell me some."

"Why yes," Hennessey said with a curt nod. "More than willing."

"Maybe I'll take you up on that. First, I need to get some wind in my face."

Clint had the saddle buckled onto Eclipse's back in record time and was settling into the familiar leather the way a hand settled into an old glove. All it took was a flick of the reins and Eclipse all but charged out of the stable.

At that moment, it seemed that neither horse nor rider could have been any happier.

THREE

Clint had thought he was tired when he got into town. That wasn't anything out of the ordinary considering all the traveling he'd been doing, but it was enough to keep his business short for the day. At least, that's what he thought when he'd first arrived.

Once he got back into the familiar saddle, however, things changed immediately. Suddenly, he felt like he didn't need a wink of sleep or more than a few quick breaths every now and then to keep himself going. Racing like the wind made him feel more alive than he had in a long time.

In fact, it didn't even feel as though he were racing like the wind. It felt more like he'd roped and saddled a whirl-wind itself and was being carried along for the wild ride of a lifetime. Judging by the steam in Eclipse's strides and the strength pouring out of every muscle, Clint wasn't the only one who was feeling good.

Man and horse worked together like they shared a single mind. Times like those made it easy to see why the Indians thought that they'd spotted some strange hybrid of man and beast when they'd first laid eyes on a mounted rider. Clint knew he didn't want to get too far out of town,

9

but actually putting that thought into action was something else entirely.

Thundering over the West Texas landscape, Clint was barely even conscious of his own self. His head and upper body hunkered down low over Eclipse's neck, moving in time to the Darley Arabian's powerful movements. His arms fell into a circular pattern of holding on to the reins while also giving them a light, occasional snap.

Even Clint's legs moved with a mind of their own. He had to alternate between urging the stallion along while also steadying himself and hanging on for dear life. It was a vital, delicate balance of tasks, but felt every bit as natural as pulling in his next breath.

One slip could have toppled him from the saddle and dropped him onto the hard, unforgiving ground.

One wrong turn could have taken them into treacherous terrain where their speed could work against them in a possibly fatal way.

But none of those things concerned them at the moment.

There were risks in walking down a street or picking a spot to make camp. Any one of them could prove fatal, but to stop doing any of that was to stop living. And at that point in time, to stop riding the whirlwind would have been like asking Clint to stop his heart from beating.

The thunder of Eclipse's hooves rumbled throughout Clint's entire body, echoing within his ears and coming to rest inside his chest. The impact of every step was absorbed effortlessly by the both of them until the movement felt like a familiar hand patting Clint on the back.

The wind enveloped them and tore at eyes and skin mercilessly, but none of that mattered. When Clint's mouth went dry, he forced himself to breathe through his nose, and when that got to be too difficult, his mouth was again ready to take over the job.

Without even knowing it, he pulled a bandanna over the lower half of his face and snapped the reins again. Eclipse

responded instantly, even though Clint couldn't rightly recall doing any of it.

All he knew was that the ride continued and they tore up
the land like a force that even nature itself had to reckon
with.

When he finally pulled back on the reins, Clint had to
take a moment to scan the horizon and figure out where
they'd ended up. A muffled laugh came from beneath his
bandanna as he brought Eclipse around to look back toward Labyrinth.

"We went a bit farther out than I'd planned, boy," Clint
said while reaching out to scratch behind the stallion's ear.
"Think we ought to turn back?"

As always, the stallion responded to Clint's voice with a
subtle shake of his head and a shifting of his hooves. Every
now and then, Clint had to wonder if the horse really did
understand him. Then again, it didn't take any sort of trick
to figure out that Eclipse would have been perfectly fine
with running full out until his legs or the ground itself gave
way beneath him.

Labyrinth wasn't much more than a bumpy ridge on
the horizon. It waited for them in the distance as though
it had been running away from them just as quickly as
they had been running away from it. When he saw the
town, Clint had to shake his head.

"Did we really go that far?" he wondered out loud. "It
seemed to me like we just got started."

Already, Eclipse was anxiously tugging at the reins in
Clint's hand. The Darley Arabian let out a few impatient
snorts while stomping lightly against the ground with one
hoof. Clint noticed that the hoof Eclipse was stomping
with was the same one that had been wrapped up and
treated with the doctor's special mixture.

Swinging down from the saddle, Clint let Eclipse calm
down a bit before kneeling to get a better look at that leg.
The memory of when that leg had been cut still made Clint

cringe. Now, the wound wasn't much more than a discoloration of skin.

"Looks like that ointment really worked," Clint said with a smile.

Eclipse looked down at him for a moment before turning his eyes back toward the trail that stretched out in front of them. Clint could feel the tension coming off of the stallion like heat radiating from his skin. More than anything, Eclipse wanted to keep going at full gallop. He just didn't seem to want to do it without Clint on his back.

"I know how you're feeling, boy. I feel the same way, but we can't go just yet. Of course," he added while climbing back into the saddle, "that doesn't mean that we can't give the wind another run for its money."

With that, Clint snapped the reins and even touched his heels to Eclipse's sides. That was more than enough to get the stallion so eager that he reared a bit before dropping his powerful legs against the ground and taking off like a bullet.

Once again, the wind built up to a roar around the pair and the ground passed beneath their feet like it was hardly even a solid thing. Clint smiled despite the dust that settled into his throat, and eventually steered Eclipse back toward town.

They arrived like a storm that had rolled in from the mountains, and the ground trembled beneath every one of their steps.

FOUR

When Clint rode back into town, he could feel that Eclipse needed to get some rest. The stallion wasn't about to slow down any time soon, but Clint could sense the fatigue that lay within the animal. It came from having been with the Darley Arabian through more tough times than he could count, and those instincts had never failed.

The stable was still open, but the liveryman was nowhere to be found. Clint didn't even concern himself with that until he'd led Eclipse back into his stall and started looking around for something to feed him. The other animals had some feed left in their own troughs and water to go with it, so the liveryman hadn't been gone for long.

"I guess he figured that we were headed out for good," Clint muttered as he started gathering something for Eclipse to eat. "Can't say as I blame him. We did take off from here like a shot."

"I'll say you did."

The statement came from the back of the stables and was immediately followed by the sound of feet rustling over the straw-covered floor. Clint shifted on the balls of his feet to turn toward the voice. His hand reflexively

13

dropped toward his gun, but stayed put before drawing the weapon.

Stepping into the faint glow of light coming from a lantern hanging from a post, the person who'd spoken gave Clint an apologetic smile. The smile was so attractive that it caught him more off his guard than her voice, which had come from nowhere.

She was a slender woman wearing work clothes that seemed to have been made for a man. The jeans and blue cotton shirt hung on her body awkwardly and were rolled up and tucked in to accommodate her shapely figure. Even with the blocky clothes, it was impossible to hide the fact that underneath them she was entirely, invitingly female.

Holding her hands up as if she were surrendering to him, the woman stepped forward a bit more. Her full red lips curled into a smile as she shook her dark blond hair over her shoulders. "I wasn't sure if I should prepare his stall for another night or if you were going to head out for a while."

Clint had relaxed by this point and was shifting on his feet in an attempt to hide the fact that he'd been startled. None of those efforts seemed to be working, so he shrugged and said, "If he had his way, I think we'd be clear across Mexico by now. Sorry about the way I turned on you like that. You managed to sneak up on me."

Smirking in a way that told Clint she knew how awkward it felt to have someone sneak up on him, the woman let it go without comment. Instead, she gave him a shrug as well. "I should be the one apologizing. I practically grew up in this stable. I know every creaky board like the back of my hand so I can move around without disturbing any of the horses."

"You grew up around here? Funny that I can't recall seeing you before. I come through Labyrinth a lot."

"Mostly I work at night," was her first explanation. Then, after a few moments ticked by, she averted her eyes and started to turn away from him. "Actually, the truth is that I know who you are."

"I hope that doesn't work against me," Clint said, half-jokingly.

"Not hardly. It's just that I know you usually take up with a few ladies around Labyrinth. The truth is that I've talked to some of them myself."

This wasn't the first time that Clint found himself stumbling into what happened when he wasn't in the room. Every man knew that women talked plenty among themselves when they were on their own. Although some men liked to poke fun at them for gossiping, the truth was that those same men probably gossiped as much as any sewing circle.

That still didn't make it any more comfortable to wander into one of those circles and get a hint that you were the subject of that gossip. Rather than show just how embarrassed he was, Clint laughed and shook his head.

"I don't think I want to hear too much more of this," he said.

Suddenly, the blonde stepped forward and held out her hands. "No, no. It's nothing like that. Well, sometimes it might be like that, but it's nothing you should be embarrassed about. Actually," she added with a little grin, "you might even be downright proud to hear some of the things they say about you."

That did it. Clint could feel the color flushing into his face and had to look away before embarrassing himself any further.

"You know, right about now the thought of riding through Mexico is looking pretty good," he said.

She laughed and stepped back so she could feed and water Eclipse. As she moved, her shapely hips shifted beneath the poorly fitted jeans, and her breasts swayed beneath the loose material of her shirt. The light from the lantern hit her just right so Clint could see the faint hint of hard little nipples poking at the rough cotton.

"This doesn't seem right," Clint said.

"What's that?"

"You know so much about me already, and I don't even know your name."

"It's Maggie," she said while reaching for a bucket of water to pour into Eclipse's trough. "Maggie Locke."

Clint reached out to take the bucket from her hands even though it was plain to see that she wasn't having a bit of trouble lifting it. "Let me help you with that, Maggie."

She glanced over at him with a knowing look on her face. As Clint's hand brushed over her own, she reached out with a few fingers as if she didn't want the brief contact to end just yet. Once the water had been poured, she took the bucket back and walked slowly toward the other side of the stable.

"That's a fine stallion you've got there," she said while looking at Clint over her shoulder.

"Thank you."

"I might get in trouble for saying this, but I tried to take him out of here while you were away."

"So that's why you work at night?" Clint asked with a dramatic menace in his voice. "To steal a man's horse when you're supposed to be watching over it?"

Maggie wasn't put off by Clint's tone in the slightest. In fact, she played into it by adding a bit of mischief into her own manner as well. "That would be easy enough to do, but I was just exercising him as ordered by Doc Hennessey."

Walking slowly toward the stacks of hay in a dark corner of the stables, Maggie looked over her shoulder every so often. Those fleeting glances might as well have been a rope tied around Clint's waist, dragging him right along behind her.

"Still, Eclipse wouldn't have any of it," she said. "He fought so hard that it made me wonder what kind of man it would take to tame a horse like that." Her voice dropped just enough for it to take on something of a smoky quality as she added, "But I already know what kind of man you are, Mr. Adams."

Clint planted his feet and stopped them both where they stood. The lantern was hanging nearby, but wasn't close enough to cast much light upon either of them.

"Oh yeah?" Clint said, sliding his hands along her sides until they came to a rest upon her hips. "And what kind of man am I?"

"The kind that wouldn't let an opportunity like this slip through his fingers."

FIVE

The stables were quiet at that time of night and the part that Clint and Maggie were in smelled like fresh hay. She kept her eyes locked on him while allowing herself to be moved back farther into the shadows. As she stepped backward, she could feel Clint's hands moving over her body, tugging at her clothes and slipping beneath them.

First, Clint's fingers slid underneath the bottom of her shirt. The contrast of the roughness of the material with the smoothness of her skin was enough to make Clint's heart speed up within his chest. Every step she took caused her hips to shift in a slow, sensual rhythm.

Next, Clint moved his thumbs along her stomach until he got them just beneath the waistband of her jeans. She pulled in a quick breath and didn't let it out until her pants were unfastened and his touch was allowed to continue down her body.

Maggie's back bumped against the wall and her eyes showed a flash of excitement. There was no place left for her to go, but there was also no other place she would rather have been. That much was obvious by the way she smiled while slowly closing her eyes and arching her back.

Clint's hands continued their downward journey, easing

18

Maggie's jeans right down along with them. As she felt her pants slide down over her hips, she shifted her weight from one foot to another until the jeans were bunched up at her ankles. From there, all she needed to do was pick up one foot and then the other to step out of the jeans altogether.

Resting on one knee in front of her, Clint took a moment to look up at Maggie. The blonde was stretched against the wall wearing nothing but the baggy men's work shirt that now looked more like a nightshirt than anything else. Her strong, naked legs came down from the shirt and the material parted just enough to give him a glimpse of the soft, downy hair between her legs.

Clint's hands were on her calves and when he eased them back up the sides of her legs, he could feel her muscles tensing beneath his fingers. She pulled in a quick breath and bit down slightly upon her bottom lip when his fingers drifted between her thighs.

He paused there and watched her face. The moment he stopped moving his hands, Clint could see a vaguely disappointed look on her face, which was quickly replaced by eager anticipation.

"Don't stop," she whispered.

Clint smiled and moved his hands up even more. By the time his fingers reached her soft little pussy, the lips were warm and wet to the touch. Leaning forward, Clint pressed his mouth against Maggie's while gently rubbing the sensitive skin between her legs.

Maggie let out a soft moan that made their kiss seem to crackle with energy. Soon, her eyes were snapping open and she was starting in on some action of her own. The first thing she did was to pull open Clint's shirt. Before she even got it off of him, she was unbuckling his belt and tugging at his pants.

They moved quickly and with a furious urgency that made every one of their movements powerful and intense. Clint's hands moved up over her hips, bunching her shirttails around her waist. By the time Clint took hold of her buttocks, Maggie had undressed him from the waist down and was practically crawling onto him.

Her legs slid up his body and wrapped around him one at a time until her ankles were locked at the small of his back. She held on to him while kissing him passionately. She was nibbling on his lip when she felt the tip of his cock rub between her legs. Opening her thighs for him just a bit more, she let out a breath while taking all of him inside.

The moment seemed to last forever. Clint felt every inch of his penis become enveloped by Maggie's smooth skin until he was buried completely inside of her. He held her off the floor with his hands cupping her bottom and her back pressed against the wall.

After a few slow strokes, Clint felt Maggie start to urge him for more by the insistent way she started to squirm against him. Not one to disappoint a lady, Clint pumped into her faster and harder. That started to bring a throaty moan from Maggie as she thrust her hips back and forth in time to his movements.

Clint took a step back from the wall, carrying Maggie along with him. When she felt that she was being held up by him alone, Maggie looked at Clint with renewed passion and started making little bites along the side of his neck.

Clint only carried her a little way before turning and lowering her onto a bed of straw lying on the floor. They were completely in the shadows now, with the rest of the stable and a partially open door not too far away. At that moment, however, neither of them was conscious of anything else. They only felt each other.

Leaning back against the straw, Maggie arched her back and spread her legs wide open while reaching out to take hold of Clint's shirt. She pulled him down onto her until he was close enough for him to kiss her on the mouth. Her tongue slipped along his lips while she once again took his cock all the way inside of her.

Still cupping the tight curves of her buttocks, Clint began pumping into her hard enough to push Maggie's back into the straw. Every time their bodies came together, Maggie let out a pleasured grunt. Her hands grasped at the straw, but were unable to find anything solid to hang on to. Once she got a hold of Clint's upper arm, she wouldn't let go.

Clint pumped into her until he could hear her breaths start to come in shallow gulps as her body writhed passionately beneath him. Every muscle pressed against him, urging him to go faster and harder with every thrust.

Finally, both of their passions exploded, climaxing to such a degree that everything else in the world seemed to blank out for a moment. There were no other sounds but the beating of their own hearts and nothing else to feel except each other's sweating, naked skin.

Clint blinked a few times and had to make an effort to steady himself. He saw that Maggie was doing the same thing and when they both finally looked at each other, they smiled widely.

Maggie looked around as though she'd only just realized where she was. "I was thinking I might get you into my bed," she whispered. "But this was even better."

"So you had this whole thing planned from the start?"

Smiling even wider, Maggie ran her fingers through Clint's tussled hair. "I know you probably think you just sweep in and women like me are powerless to resist, but you're not the only one with sinful thoughts. Does that disappoint you?"

"Not hardly. Actually," Clint added while sliding his hands up and down Maggie's bare hips, "it sounds pretty damn good coming from you."

Her eyes narrowed and she savored the feel of his hands on her body for a few moments before opening them again.

Their bodies were still joined and Maggie moved one leg slowly up and down Clint's side. Her flat stomach moved with every breath, leading back up into the shirt, which had been bunched up in the heat of the moment. Just looking at the way she was half-dressed and lying beneath him made Clint feel ready to pick up right where they'd left off.

"But be honest," Clint said. "There was a bit of sweeping done on my part."

She kept her eyes open, but started to laugh under her breath. "I guess you could say that."

Before Clint could get in any sort of boast, she pulled him down and planted a kiss on his mouth. Once again, they rolled back into the shadows.

SIX

It had been a long time since Clint had slept so well. In fact, when he was awakened by the first rays of the sun pouring through his hotel window, he thought he could roll over and pass out again. All it took was a few breaths of fresh air for him to change his mind about that, however, and he was soon dressed and ready to go.

His muscles were sore from so many kinds of exertion that he thought he might have done all of the previous day's running himself. When he went in to check on Eclipse, he saw that he wasn't the only one feeling the effects from the day before.

The Darley Arabian was sleeping soundly and barely even shifted when Clint came by to have a look at him. Rather than wake the stallion, Clint left the stables and headed off to try and find some breakfast. He knew of several places to go, but decided to make one more stop before filling his belly. Turning at the next corner, Clint walked toward Rick's Place.

As Clint walked down the street, it felt as if the entire town was coming awake to greet him. Doors and shutters opened and faces peeked out to get their look at the new day. Plenty of those faces were familiar, and Clint acknowledged them with a nod or a wave.

With all the traveling he did, it was an awfully good feeling to know that he had a place like Labyrinth to call his home. The only feeling better than that was actually being in that same place for a while. As much as Clint enjoyed riding free from one end of the country to the other, it did him a whole lot of good to walk down streets that he could navigate just as well with his eyes shut.

Already, Clint was picking out what he was going to order from a menu that hadn't changed since the first time he'd laid eyes on it. Even now, he could feel the rickety chair beneath him and could hear the squeaks coming from floorboards that had needed to be repaired for well over a decade.

All of those details brought a smile to his face. That smile faded, however, when he got a look at the men who had turned a corner to walk in the same direction he was.

The men weren't too off-putting all by themselves. There were less than half a dozen of them in all and not one of them was especially big. They were average height and dressed like any number of cowboys who came strutting in off the range with money in their pockets and fire in their eyes.

Three things separated these men from any other group that might be out carousing in a town like Labyrinth. First of all, it was too early to carouse anywhere. Second, the group was too tightly knit to be just a group of friends. Three, every last one of them were heeled.

That last detail caught Clint's attention the most. Not only that, but his practiced senses told Clint that the men in his sights right now were very comfortable with the guns hanging at their sides. It wasn't anything specific that tipped him off. It was more of a vague feeling that came from his gut, which was hardly ever wrong.

Without having to think much of it, Clint waited for the

group of men to get a little farther in front of him before falling into step behind them. He watched them like a hawk, but did it in a way that seemed innocent enough. Whenever one of the cowboys would occasionally take a quick look behind them, Clint's eyes were always focused on something else while the expression on his face was lackadaisical at best. All the while, his steps were slow and easy. His hand was close to his gun, but simply because his thumbs were hooked over his belt.

Of course, if things got bad enough, Clint could get to his gun in the blink of an eye no matter where his hands were.

For some men, that might have been a boast. For Clint Adams, it was simple fact.

Even though they checked behind them every now and then, the men still seemed pretty much confident that there wasn't anything for them to worry about. There was a moment, however, when Clint realized that he'd fallen into that same trap himself.

Just when he was thinking that he had everything well enough in hand, Clint started closing the distance between himself and the group of armed men. The whole parade was getting closer to Rick's Place and Clint wasn't too comfortable with that many overconfident guns being so close to his friend's saloon.

Clint knew he hadn't been picked out of the crowd yet and guessed that the group wasn't about to pick him out anytime soon. His own overconfidence was apparent when one of the men at the head of the group turned and not only looked behind him, but looked directly at Clint.

Because Clint had picked up his own pace to keep the five men in his sight, he now had nowhere to go when the other man's eyes fell onto him. There were no shadows or doorways that he could get to without diving headfirst.

All Clint could do was lower his head, cover his face with the brim of his hat, and hope that was enough to do the trick.

Clint wasn't able to see enough of the group to know if they'd looked away from him or not, but his senses were stretching out until they strained him. Finally, Clint got the feeling that he was no longer being scrutinized and gave it another second or two before looking up again.

Sure enough, the men had shifted their eyes forward and were walking down the side of the street like a unit marching into war. No matter if they'd seen him or not, Clint didn't like the looks of these men one bit. And the more he watched them, the tighter the knot in the pit of his stomach became.

After another few seconds, Clint didn't even have to guess where the men were headed. His worst-case scenario was playing out; the men were obviously headed for Rick's. Not only that, but they seemed to be firing themselves up as though they expected blood to be spilled when they got there.

More than that, it seemed they expected to be the ones doing the spilling.

All thoughts of keeping himself hidden went out of Clint's mind. It was too late to head them off, and Clint doubted that would have done him much good anyhow. If he'd learned one thing for certain after watching the group of five for this short amount of time, it was that they weren't about to be distracted by anything less than an act of God.

Of course, that didn't mean that Clint was about to run up and tap them on the shoulder. If anything, that would probably just put them more on edge than they already were. The only thing worse for Rick than having some armed men storming into his place would be for those armed men to be all riled up before they even got there.

No, Clint decided to hang back and keep the men in his sights for the moment. At least that way, he wouldn't be the one responsible for stirring up a hornet's nest. Then again, it seemed as though the hornets were already plenty stirred already.

Clint shook his head as the five men pushed open the door to Rick's Place and strutted inside. He could already hear the voices full of piss and vinegar thundering within the saloon. Keeping his hand down close to his modified Colt, Clint headed for the saloon to see just what the hell this was all about.

SEVEN

"Aw, Jesus," Rick muttered when he saw what was headed toward his front door. "Just what the hell do these jokers want?"

The person he'd been talking to was a young girl who served drinks. She was a pretty brunette with eyes that betrayed a wisdom slightly beyond her twenty-some years. She gave Hartman a knowing smirk, but made sure the expression was gone by the time she turned around to look at the saloon's newest arrivals.

She wasn't the only one to put on a different face. Rick Hartman had shifted his smile from sarcastic to vaguely genuine by the time the front door was slammed open. All five men filed in through the entrance, making sure that every last one of their steps echoed like thunder.

"What can I do for you gentlemen?" Rick asked.

The man at the front of the pack was a burly fellow with hair as black as a raven's wing and a hooked, beaklike nose to go along with it. His eyes burned with an inner fire and his rough, Mediterranean features formed an angry mask that covered his entire face. After taking a few steps into the saloon, he stopped where he was, knowing full well that everyone else would just have to walk around him.

Once his men had settled in around and behind him, the man with the black hair shifted his eyes and had a look around before settling his gaze onto Rick. In a gruff baritone, he boomed, "You know damn well why we're here, Hartman."

"Yeah," chimed in another of the five. He was smaller than the rest and seemed to hover around the bigger fellas the way a fly never strayed too far from a pile of shit. "You know why we're here."

The remaining men kept quiet, but the violent promises in their eyes said plenty to anyone with the guts to look directly into them.

Rick Hartman was one such man. Even so, he didn't have to see the meanness in those men's eyes to know it was there. He'd seen it plenty of other times recently. But he didn't give the men one hint of what he was thinking. The smile was still on his face, refusing to give his visitors the satisfaction of knowing they might be getting under his skin.

"If you'd care for a drink, the first round would be on me," Rick said with his beaming smile still firmly in place.

The big man at the head of the pack wore a long, dark coat that hung over broad shoulders. As his hands ran down the edges of the coat, they lingered near the double-rig holster strapped around his waist. "We didn't come here to drink," he said. "But if we did, you'd sure as hell better not charge us a cent."

"Yeah," the smaller gunman said. "You better not."

Hartman took in the sight before him, ignoring the sneering face of the smallest gunman. That one had already been written off as more bluster than brains in Rick's book. As for the others, he knew better than to write any of them off just yet.

"Then why don't you save us all a lot of time and say what's on your mind, Paul?" Rick said. "You're making my customers nervous."

Although none of the customers who'd already been in Rick's Place wanted to look that way, they couldn't help but cringe a bit under the gunmen's roving stares. The women stared back defiantly, only faltering when one of the gunmen started sizing them up as though they were one of the daily specials.

His hand slowly wandering beneath the bar, Rick spoke up loud enough to draw all of the attention back to himself. "If you intend on scaring me into paying you, you've got another thing coming."

"Oh, do I now?" The biggest of the bunch, Paul, kept his hands close to his double rig and took a few more steps into the saloon. "And what's gonna stop me from just coming in here and taking what's rightfully mine?"

Rick's hand was inching closer and closer to the shotgun secreted under the bar. "Nothing," he said. "Except the only thing here that's rightfully yours is that free drink I offered. Keep up this behavior and that offer will dry up as well."

Although nobody in the place wanted to say anything at that moment, none of the other customers were brave enough to move either. Instead, they all stayed where they were as if they'd suddenly sprouted roots and tried to act as though they simply preferred to stay quiet.

"Everyone else has been paying," Paul said. "What makes you think you're so damn special?"

"I don't think I'm special. I just don't think I'll be paying you a damn thing."

"You should've thought about that before you went and ran up a debt, then. Now it's too late to do anything about it." Paul took another step and the other four men around him drifted into the saloon right along with him. "Now, you've only got two choices left. Pay up or die."

Rick's eyes narrowed as his fingers settled around the grip of the shotgun. The weapon was of the smaller variety that was made to fit in small places. The barrel had been filed down to less than a foot in length and the handle had been whittled down until it was only slightly bigger than the handle of a pistol.

"Then it seems like you've got a problem here," Rick said in a low, deadly tone. "Because I'm not about to do either one of those things."

Just then, it seemed as though all the men around Paul had been waiting to hear those very words come from Hartman's mouth. They fanned out until they formed a firing line that practically took up the entire front portion of the saloon. Every one of those men rested their hands upon their own weapons as if daring Hartman to say one more word they didn't like. The expressions on their faces made it perfectly obvious that they wanted nothing more than to get just such an invitation to draw.

Paul leered at Hartman and nodded slowly. His men moved around him like the gears of a well-oiled machine. Even the smallest of the bunch fell into position without a moment's hesitation. The door was blocked and everyone inside the saloon was well within the gunmen's sights.

There was no escaping unless someone wanted to walk straight down Paul's throat.

"You sure about that?" Paul asked smugly. "Because from where I'm standing it don't look like you can back up a goddamn word you just said."

EIGHT

Rick leaned forward as though he was supporting his weight with his hands upon the edge of his bar. The truth of the matter was that he was standing that way so he could keep ahold of his shotgun without bringing the weapon into the open. Another truth was that he didn't dare make a move with the weapon since he was already covered from five different angles.

"I'm gettin' real sick of you, Hartman," Paul said. "Folks around here tend to honor their debts. And for certain, they know better than to give lip to me and my boys."

"That is unless they want their lips blown clean off their face," the smallest of the bunch chimed in.

Paul nodded and smirked at the comment. "That's right, Zack. Which type of man do you think ol' Rick Hartman is? The kind that honors his debts or the kind that puts his own head on the chopping block?"

Rick's hand was on the shotgun and his finger was touching the trigger. He wasn't stupid or impetuous, however, which meant that he still was a long way from thinking that he had any kind of edge in this situation. Although he wasn't about to pull the shotgun just yet, he wasn't exactly going to let his hand stray from the weapon either.

"Come on, Rick," Paul said as his eyes flickered to a spot peculiarly close to the shotgun Rick was hiding. "Why don't you show us which kind of man you are?"

Hartman wavered for a moment before finally allowing himself to draw a breath. "Well, I can tell you one thing for certain. I know I'm the kind of man that has good friends in the right places."

Paul's brow furrowed as he tried to make sense out of what he'd just heard. The statement had been so unexpected that it seemed to send a pain right through the big man's temple. "What's that supposed to mean?"

"You heard him," Clint said as he made his presence known.

Even though he filled up a good portion of the doorway, Clint hadn't made a sound when he'd approached. He'd arrived like a shadow, brushing over the boards on the floor without raising a single eyebrow along the way.

Since Paul was the one closest to the door, Clint was right behind him when he stepped in. Paul started to turn around, but stopped when he heard the sound of iron brushing against leather and felt a barrel jab him in the ribs.

Paul twitched, but not enough for Clint to see it from where he was standing. His entire body went rigid as a board and even his breaths became slow and steady.

"I take it yer the friend he was talking about," Paul said.

"That's right," Clint replied. "And I sure am in the right place."

Slowly, Paul twisted his head around so he could take a look over his shoulder. He couldn't see much, but he did see enough to satisfy his curiosity. "Thought so," he said. "You'd be the high and mighty Clint Adams."

"I don't know about the rest of it, but you got my name right."

"Funny. I didn't know you were the type of man to sneak up on someone and put a gun in his back."

"Only when there's no alternative."

Suddenly, Paul seemed to forget that the Colt was even drawn. He looked around at his men and raised his voice until it was loud enough to echo off the walls. "Well, my boys ain't about to shoot no one. Why don't you come inside and join us?" Lowering his voice to a mean rasp, he added, "Or would you just prefer to kill an unarmed man like a damn yellow coward?"

Clint moved the Colt away from Paul's ribs and dropped it back into its holster without making a sound. The next thing Paul felt was the slap of Clint's hand on his shoulder. The impact was loud enough to make the armed men jump, but not as high as Paul when he felt that sudden smack.

Pushing Paul aside as he walked past him, Clint stepped into the saloon as though he meant to make himself comfortable. "I guess since all you want to do is talk, then I can be just as reasonable."

The smaller of the men fidgeted and shifted on his feet once he got a good look at Clint. His fingers flexed and he nervously licked his lips. Finally, it got to the point where it seemed as though he was going to burst if he didn't make some sort of move.

His hand dropped toward his gun as Clint walked by. Before he could clear leather, he heard a familiar brushing sound and then heard the metallic snap of a hammer being thumbed back. When he looked up again, the smaller guy was looking straight down the barrel of Clint's modified Colt.

Smirking from the other end of that barrel, Clint gave the smaller guy a quick nod. "And here I thought we were going to be sociable."

"Relax, Zack," Paul said. "If Mr. Adams wants to be a good boy, we got no grudge against him. Our problem is with Hartman over there."

Grudgingly, Zack moved his hand away from his holster. Only when the fight went out of his eyes did he see the Colt move in the slightest.

Clint lowered the pistol and holstered it. He could feel the hairs on his arms and the back of his neck stand on end as if the air were charged with lightning. He kept his posture and expression relaxed, however, as he made his way to the bar and leaned against it. The spot he'd chosen was close enough to Rick that he could whisper to Hartman without being heard by anyone else.

"What's going on here?" Clint asked.

Rick let out a sigh, but knew better than to take his eyes off of the unwelcome visitors. "Just some nasty business that's been brewing since you've been away."

"How nasty?"

"Let's just say I'm the one that's getting the least trouble from these assholes."

"I hate to say it, Rick, but that looks like it's about to change real quickly."

NINE

"This don't have to be so rough," Paul said to Rick. "All you need to do is pay what you owe us."

"I hate to come in at the middle like this," Clint said, "but what exactly does Rick owe you?"

"No more than anyone else around here."

Clint's eyes narrowed and he focused them on Paul. "Is this some sorry excuse for a protection scheme?"

Paul laughed once and shook his head. "Not hardly." His laughter stopped just as quickly as it started and his voice suddenly took on a deadly serious tone. "But I'm not in the habit of explaining myself to people who poke their noses in where they don't belong, neither. So just do yourself a favor, Mister Gunsmith, and talk to your friend some other time."

"Yeah," Zack chimed in with a smile. "Some other time." As he spoke, the smaller man stepped forward and made a reach for his gun. His lips curled back in a defiant sneer and he kept right on drawing until he was about to clear leather.

Clint let him get that far just to make sure the guy was seriously trying to do something after all that had happened. When he saw that Zack truly had somehow gotten a burr under his saddle that was big enough to make him draw, Clint knew he had to do something about it.

Clint hated drawing his gun unless he was going to use it and he'd done that twice already. So rather than draw his own Colt, he stepped forward in a rush of motion that carried him across the floor like a trap that had been sprung. He reached out with one hand so quickly that he managed to dig his fingers between Zack's hand and his gun. From there, Clint was able to take the other man's weapon for himself and pluck it clean out of his possession.

The other three men that had come in with Paul looked as though they'd just seen a miracle. It took them a moment or two to realize what Clint had done. Before they could do anything about it, Zack was disarmed and sputtering in disbelief.

Clint wasn't about to stand around and wait to see what the other men were going to do. While he'd taken the gun away from Zack, he'd been glancing around to see what the others were up to. For the moment, Paul wasn't making a single move. The other three, however, weren't so smart.

One of those others, a balding man with a big rounded gut, was trying to draw his pistol as fast as he could. That attempt at speed made him sloppy and his hand fumbled a few times against the side of his holster before he even managed to touch steel. That fumbling only got worse when he saw that Clint was headed straight for him.

Another of Paul's men stood just an inch or two shorter than Clint. That one had already drawn his weapon and was bringing it up to aim. Clint's eye was trained enough to see the trembling in the man's hand. Although he managed to squeeze off the first shot, the shot was so rushed that it didn't even manage to hit the large mirror hanging behind the bar.

That only left one more fellow. This one stood a few inches taller than Clint and he seemed more angry than anything else. He was a bit slower on the draw, but had a

steadier hand. He saw Clint turn in his direction and make
a move with his gun hand before being able to point his
own weapon that way.

Although Clint had made his move, it wasn't the kind of
move the bigger man was expecting. Clint's arm snapped
back and then straight out again like a whip being cracked.
At the end of the snap, he opened his grip and allowed
Zack's gun to go spinning outward toward the bigger man.

Just as the big man was about to pull his trigger, the flying gun caught him square on the nose and sent a blinding
flash of pain through his entire head. He was so disoriented
that his legs began to wobble beneath him. His finger
clenched around his trigger, but sent his round into the side
of the bar, just missing the top of a spittoon resting near the
foot rail.

Clint planted his foot, but continued moving toward the
fat man. Just as the man with the big gut had managed to get
a grip on his weapon, he felt something take his breath away
and send a wave of nausea through him. The something that
he'd felt was Clint's boot being driven right up into his belly.

With the fat man already doubling over and the bigger
one reeling from the pain of his busted nose, Clint dropped
his hand down to his Colt and fixed his eyes on the shorter
gunman who'd already missed with his first shot.

The shorter gunman had his pistol in hand and his finger on the trigger. Although that meant his body was ready
to take another shot, that didn't mean the rest of him was
so eager. His eyes blinked in a quick flutter and his breathing started to speed up. His hand was trembling so much
that anyone in the saloon had an equal chance of getting hit
if he found the stones to pull his trigger.

"Come on now," Clint warned. "Don't force this to go
any further."

For a moment, there was silence.

Then, sounds started to filter through the air one by one,
like bats fluttering from a cave.

First, a worried whimper came from one of the customers in the saloon. Next, people started to fidget nervously in their seats as they tried to decide if they should sit still or make a run for the door. Finally, there was a muffled thump as the end of Rick's shotgun bumped against the bar while he brought it up to hold at just over waist level.

"All right, all right. This has gone far enough."

Oddly enough, that statement hadn't come from Clint or Rick.

It came from Paul, who held out his hands toward his men as though he were simply trying to defuse a minor scuffle. He didn't even seem to notice all the iron being waved around as he walked up and placed both hands flat upon the bar.

"You'll have to excuse my boys," he said to both Clint and Rick. "They tend to get a little worked up sometimes."

"I'm plenty worked up right now," Clint said. "How about you do something to change this before it heads even further south?"

"All right," Paul said with a nod. He then lifted a hand and snapped his fingers.

All of the other men took a few moments to respond, but they eventually started lowering their guns. Once they saw that Clint was doing the same, the gunmen holstered their pistols and backed away. That is, most of them backed away.

The biggest of the bunch was still shaky on his feet and managed to wobble sideways until he found a chair he could drop himself onto. Sucking in a wheezing breath, the gunman with the gut hanging over his holster was only just able to pull in a full breath. When he did, he let it out with a pained grunt.

Paul smiled warmly and shifted his eyes back toward Rick. "There. Happy?"

"I'll be happy once you take your men out of my place. None of you are welcome here no more."

That brought a little twitch to Paul's eye, but he held his tongue before spitting out his reply. After a glance in Clint's direction, he slapped the top of the bar and took a step back. "Fine. But don't think that this means you get to cut out of your obligations." Focusing on Clint, he added, "As for you . . . we've got business between us now. I'll be seeing you to collect soon enough."

Before anything else could be said, Paul turned and walked out of the saloon. His men filed out behind him, with Zack leading the way so closely that he nearly tripped on Paul's heels.

When the others were gone, Clint leaned against the bar and said, "First, I want a beer. Second, I want to know what the hell was going on here."

TEN

For a moment, it seemed that Rick was going to lose a whole lot of business. As soon as the gunmen saw their way out of the saloon, several of the customers flew out of there as well. The rest of them stayed put and began to talk excitedly among themselves about what they'd seen. For those folks, seeing a saloon brawl was the whole reason they'd come to Texas in the first place.

Rick didn't even notice the people who left. By the time he'd squared things away and poured a beer for himself and Clint, enough people had come in to replace the ones who had scattered. Then again, it seemed as though Rick wouldn't have cared too much if the entire place had cleared out and stayed that way.

"I appreciate what you did for me, Clint," Rick said after draining a good portion of his beer. "You always know when to show up."

Clint lifted his mug and said, "Then here's to sticking my nose into other people's business."

Apparently, Rick wasn't the only one to appreciate that comment. That much was obvious simply because Hartman wasn't the only one to lift his glass. Several of the

41

customers who'd been there the whole time lifted theirs as well and gave Clint an approving wave to go along with it.

Seeing that brought a smile to Rick's face and even got him to laugh a bit. It wasn't long though before a shadow crept in at the corners of his eyes.

"Those didn't look like the type you normally cater to in here," Clint said. "And they didn't seem to appreciate your hospitality."

"No, Paul doesn't appreciate much of anything besides money in his pockets."

Clint wanted to hear more, but knew that Rick would tell him in good time. Despite the anxiety churning in his belly, Clint took another sip of his beer and waited for his friend to get around to the task at hand. He didn't have to wait for more than another couple of seconds.

"His name's Paul Castiglione," Rick explained. "I know a few of them others by name, but I doubt you'd recognize any of them."

After thinking it over for a moment, Clint shrugged. "Can't say as I've heard of Paul Castiglione either."

"Then I'm certain you wouldn't recognize any of those others' names. Most of those hired guns are from around here and haven't done much besides steal some horses or break a few legs."

"What about Paul? It seems to me that he's done worse than that."

Rick let out a single laugh that didn't have a trace of humor in it. He sipped his beer and then set it down. When he looked up at Clint, he simply nodded. "Yeah. He's done a lot worse than that."

After all the years they'd been friends, Clint didn't need to hear much more than that to know what was on Hartman's mind. He could read a lot into a man just by looking into his eyes. That much came from knowing his way around a poker table.

In this case, Clint could practically read Rick's mind

just by listening to what he said and how he said it. That much came from sticking with Hartman through thick and thin.

"He says you owe him," Clint pointed out. "Is that true?"

"Well, that depends."

"Depends on what?"

"On whether or not you're willing to buy into what he's selling." Hartman took another sip of his beer and then walked over to refill both his and Clint's glasses. Seeing that Clint was getting short on patience, he quickly added, "It goes like this. Paul Castiglione works for a bunch of washed-up prospectors who tried to get rich by panning or digging for gold, silver, or whatever they could find. When that didn't work out, him and his partners started stealing from more successful prospectors."

"Not a good way to make a living, but not all that uncommon."

"True. Things get rough when you take a bunch of dirt-poor, hungry men and then throw them out in the brush for weeks at a time to live among themselves and the coyotes. They start chewing at each other. Add the fact that they weren't all that good to begin with into the mix and you've got some real trouble."

"We're a long way from any mines, Rick," Clint said as a way to prod his friend along a little more.

Rick accepted the comment with a nod. "Yeah, but we're a hell of a lot closer to anything that might pay off than Paul or his boys ever got. That is, until they stumbled upon a fellow by the name of Loren Janes."

Squinting, Clint said. "Loren Janes? I think I've heard that name before."

"Wouldn't be surprised if you had. Loren Janes is a big investor around here. He's probably funded half of the businesses that were started in West Texas. He's a good man." Taking a sip of his beer, Rick added, "Or I should say he was a good man."

"What happened to him?"

"He wanted to get out and get his hands dirty instead of sitting behind a desk. At least, that's how the story goes. What is pretty obvious now is that he got out in the open territory and ran into some bad men along the way."

"Paul Castiglione," Clint said.

"You got it. My guess is that Paul and his boys didn't even really know what they'd stumbled into until all the smoke had cleared. What I can say for certain is that they left here with next to nothing and they came back with some very important papers clutched in their mangy hands."

"Papers?"

"I know," Rick said with a snorting laugh. "Seems hardly feasible that they can even read. But they got some things from Mr. Janes that gives them rightful ownership to most of the land in Labyrinth."

The bottom of Clint's stomach dropped a bit closer to his boots. While he'd been expecting to hear some bad news, he wasn't quite prepared for something like that. He froze with his hands on the bar. It took a moment for him to realize that he was almost staring with his jaw hanging open.

"Just how did that happen?" Clint asked. "How could he have gotten something like that? I mean, that's not exactly the kind of thing a man travels with."

Rick looked back at Clint, shaking his head as though he still couldn't believe any of it either. "He says he got the documents from Janes legally and there isn't any proof otherwise. He's got them, though, and they're legitimate. I should know since I paid a lawyer to check them out myself."

"What did the lawyer say?"

"That they were the real papers. There was even a contract signing them over from Janes to Paul."

"Would Janes do something like that?"

Rick gave Clint a look that said he was surprised that

Clint would even ask. "Why on earth would he do that?"

Clint shook his head. He had just been thinking out loud, but even he'd seen the flaw in his logic before his words were fresh out of his mouth. "So what's this money he says you owe him?"

"Rent," Hartman stated. "Collecting on a mortgage that should be getting paid off in a few more years. Foreclosing. You think of some sort of legal term for squeezing us for money and Paul's used it already. Nearly everyone in town owes Janes for land, rent, or to pay back some sort of loan. Now that Paul's got his hands on those contracts, he's got all of us by the short hairs and he means to collect as much as he can as quickly as he can."

"Yeah," Clint said. "We'll just see about that."

ELEVEN

Clint didn't have much use for lawyers.

It wasn't anything personal; he just simply rarely found an occasion to visit one. Normally, they were used for proposing contracts or settling disputes. Most of Clint's contracts were through a man's good word and most of his disputes were settled with iron and lead. Although Clint's way wasn't as civil as a lawyer's, it suited him a whole lot better. Also, he didn't have to muck around in courtrooms.

Alright, maybe he did dislike lawyers just a bit. There was just something about the way they took an hour to say the simplest thing. And while they were taking that hour, they were doing their best to make a man look foolish through a bunch of fancy words.

Clint knew plenty of good words himself, but that still never seemed to do much good against a lawyer who made it his business to shoot holes in anything that was said the way Buffalo Bill might shoot holes through a wooden target.

On second thought, Clint had to admit that he liked lawyers even less than he'd thought. By the time he'd made it to the plain building on the corner of Second Avenue, he shrugged and decided that he was just fine with that little bit of prejudice.

Clint made his way down the street toward the office of Harold Meyer, Attorney-at-Law. Despite the less than flattering things rolling through his mind, Clint put on a pleasant face and stepped into the lawyer's office. The place smelled like a dusty library and looked about as appealing as a dried-up river bed.

But there was at least one thing in the office that made Clint want to stay. It was the desk toward the back of the small room used as a reception area. Actually, the desk was just as plain as everything else. It was the slim brunette behind the desk that caught Clint's eye.

When she looked up at him, she was prepared to be bothered by yet another person seeking legal counsel. That expectation was plain enough to see by the bored expression on her face. A pleasantly surprised smile replaced the frown the moment she got a look at who'd stepped into the office.

"Well hello there," she said cheerily. "What can I do for you?"

The brunette looked to be in her mid-twenties. Her hair was coal black and hung in thick, straight strands to well below her shoulder blades. Thin, pink lips curled into a smile and light green eyes fixed upon Clint with more than a little interest. She wore a simple purple dress with a black ribbon tied around her neck.

Clint stepped up to the desk and took a look around. It was his natural instinct to observe his surroundings. Even though he and the brunette seemed to be the only living things in sight, he didn't relax until he'd checked every corner for himself.

"Good afternoon," Clint said while returning her smile. "I'm here to see Harold Meyer. Is he in?"

For a moment, the brunette didn't seem to want to answer

the question. She was too busy taking in the sight of Clint to be worried about things like her job. With a sigh, she nodded. "He's here. There's not a lot of other places he would be."

The boredom in her voice was as plain as the cute little nose on her face. Come to think of it, the rest of her wasn't half bad to look at, either. Although the dress was cut in a conservative manner, it couldn't completely hide the brunette's small, pert breasts or her trim figure. Another thing that couldn't be hidden was the joy that she got when she caught Clint looking at her so carefully.

Actually, the brunette didn't even try to hide that.

"Do you have an appointment?" she asked, even as her eyes wandered up and down Clint's body.

"No, but I was hoping I could get in to see him anyway. My name's Clint Adams and I'm a friend of—"

"Rick Hartman," she said as her eyes suddenly widened. "I've heard him mention you."

"Nothing bad, I hope."

"Not too bad, anyway." After a pause and a quick look over her shoulder, she said, "Mr. Meyer usually likes to schedule all his business, but I don't see any reason why you can't see him. It's not like he's too busy right now."

"I didn't catch your name, ma'am."

"It's Kara."

"Well, I appreciate your help, Kara."

"Quite all right. If I catch any hell for letting you go in, I expect you to make it up to me."

"I like the sound of that. But do I need for him to get angry for that?"

"Not at all."

Tipping his hat, Clint walked on by the desk. "Then I'll be checking in on you a little later."

The brunette watched him for as long as she could until Clint had walked past her desk. Rather than turn in her chair to keep him in her sight, she found something to do where she was and smiled to herself. She started to hum a tune that filled the dusty air within the small front room and all the way down the hall to a pair of doors situated side by side.

Clint had just arrived at those doors himself when he stopped and took a look at them. One had a sign that was marked with the name of a local land surveyor and the other bore the name of Harold Meyer written in black, blocky letters.

Knocking on the door, Clint opened it and stepped inside. That one step was all that was needed to take the smile off his face that Kara had put there and remind him of why he hadn't been looking forward to this visit in the first place.

The air was thicker than the dust on the most obscure law book at the back of one of the dozen shelves lining the office's walls. The smell of dry parchment, ink, and cigar smoke permeated the room. In the middle of it sat a squat, round-faced man with a head sprouting a crop of bushy black hair.

"Do you have an appointment?" the man asked in an annoyed tone.

"No, but I just needed a moment of your time."

"My time is very valuable. That's why I normally require an appointment."

"It's about Paul Castiglione."

Judging by the way the lawyer's face immediately paled, Clint knew he'd come to the right place.

TWELVE

Although the lawyer tried to maintain his aggravated demeanor, he was sputtering too much to hold it up for very long. Having stood up when Clint entered his office, the squat man lowered himself back into his chair and grabbed for the cigar box sitting on the edge of his desk.

Clint stepped forward and was able to take a seat for himself before the cigar reached the other man's lips. In fact, Clint was able to cross his legs, dig a match from his pocket, strike it, and offer it toward the lawyer's cigar before the other man could even get himself to stop trembling.

"Um, thank you," the man said as he leaned forward and lit his cigar from the flame grasped between Clint's fingers. Pulling in some of the cigar's smoke had a calming effect. When he puffed the smoke back out again, the man seemed almost collected.

"Nervous?" Clint asked at just the right moment.

The man's eyes shifted and he slid his backside against his chair. "Nervous? Me? Why do you ask?"

Clint put out the match with a flick of his wrist and then flipped the charred stick into the tin tray on the desk. As he did this, he fixed a knowing smirk on his face and said,

"You may be a great lawyer, but you should never play poker."

The man across the desk from Clint laughed nervously and nodded. "I guess hearing that name does provoke a reaction in most folks around here. Especially lately."

"That's what I wanted to ask you about," Clint said.

Now that he had his cigar going, the lawyer seemed more at ease. "Of course, so long as you're here. What's your relation with Mr. Castiglione?"

"I'm Clint Adams. I'm a friend of Rick Hartman's, and my only relation with Castiglione is that he seemed about ready to throw a punch at me not too long ago."

While that seemed to strike a chord with the lawyer, it didn't appear to be a particularly bad chord. Nodding while puffing on the cigar, he said, "Harold Meyer," without extending a hand. "Pleased to make your acquaintance Mr. Adams. I know you frequent Labyrinth. Amazing we've never met."

Normally, Clint liked to be called by his first name. From this one, however, Mr. Adams seemed much more appropriate.

"I've been talking to Rick Hartman and he said that this Castiglione fellow has some sort of legal claim to some of the local businesses?"

"Perfectly legal," Meyer said with a nod. "I went over the papers and contracts myself."

"From what I heard, a man by the name of Loren Janes is the one who holds those contracts."

"They've been signed over. Like I said, perfectly legal."

"Doesn't that strike you as a bit peculiar?" Clint asked.

"Peculiar? How so?"

Leaning back in his chair, Clint watched Meyer to make sure the other man wasn't trying to pull one over on him. Now that the lawyer seemed to be on more familiar territory, his face had become all but a blank, expressionless mask.

"Peculiar because signing over those contracts is like Janes handing over most of his income," Clint said. "At least, that's how I read it. Besides, it seemed that Janes wasn't the sort of man to put the people he did business with in this type of situation."

"You know Mr. Janes?"

"Not personally, but Rick speaks highly of him."

"Then perhaps you should reserve your judgment until you get your facts straight, Mr. Adams."

"I think I have pretty good judgment. So does Rick Hartman and he's done enough business with Janes to get a read on his character."

Shrugging while rolling the cigar in his mouth, Meyer kicked his feet up onto his desk and said, "Reading someone's character and off-the-cuff judgments are hardly facts. You seem like you'd be intelligent enough to know that, Mr. Adams."

Not only could Clint tell at that moment that he wasn't going to get a damn thing out of Meyer, but he was also reminded of why he generally liked stepping on snakes and getting splinters more than talking to lawyers. Rather than show any of that, he did his best to maintain his cordial smile and nodded.

"Any chance I could get a look at those contracts?" Clint asked.

"Any chance that you've signed any of those contracts?"

Clint shook his head.

"Then no, Mr. Adams. There's no chance of you seeing them."

"Any chance you know how much grief Castiglione has been giving to folks around here because of those contracts?"

Again, Meyer shrugged.

Clint leaned forward until it looked as though he were about to pounce over the desk and jump down Meyer's throat. "What's the law say about Castiglione coming into town and demanding money from honest business owners?"

"What are they supposed to say? It's all legal, Mr. Adams. Are Mr. Castiglione's practices unsavory? Yes. Can I do anything about them? No."

"Not when he's your client, right?"

Meyer nodded. "That's right."

Suddenly, Meyer's eyebrows arched and he cocked his head like a confused dog. "How did you know I was representing Castiglione on some of his matters?"

"I didn't," Clint said as he stood up and headed for the door. "Not until you told me just now."

It was an old trick, but sometimes those were the best kind when used at the proper times. Clint savored the genuine frustration building up behind the lawyer's eyes. "Don't worry, counselor, it happens to the best of us."

"You want some free advice, Mr. Adams?"

Clint stopped with his hand holding the door open and turned to look back at Meyer's desk. "That's the best kind."

"Keep out of this. It's too late for me, but not for you."

As far as Clint could tell, the lawyer was being perfectly up-front just then. That, more than anything, surprised him.

THIRTEEN

It wasn't until almost suppertime that Clint stepped back into Rick's Place. At that time of day, the saloon was doing a good business, and the air was filled with the sounds of conversation, laughter, bottles knocking together, and even the occasional back hitting the floor.

Although Rick made sure to run a good place, that didn't mean he was going to step in when some of his customers were having fun. A few young men near the bar were roughhousing a bit, but toned it down once they saw the stern glare coming from the saloon's owner. That glare turned into a beaming smile when it was shifted toward the front door.

"Clint! There you are. I was beginning to think you rode off with some pretty lady."

Stepping up to the bar, Clint shook his head and replied, "That's not until a little later. Right now, I'd like to have another word with you."

"Sure thing. You hungry?"

"Of course."

"Then let me have something whipped up for the both of us and we can talk over that. Sound good?"

"Sure, just so long as it's better than the last meal you

54

served me. I've got a bad enough taste in my mouth already, so I don't need anything else adding to it."

Rick winced sympathetically. "What's the matter? You been digging into this mess with Castiglione?"

Rolling his eyes, Clint nodded and waited for Rick to step out from behind the bar. When his friend was leading him toward an empty table, Clint said, "You called it right. I've been all over town, but most recently at the office of public records. You weren't kidding when you said that Castiglione owns half of Labyrinth. I'd say he owns most of it."

"Yep. I talked to some lawyers over on Fourth Street about them contracts. They might be able to tell you all the details."

"Already did that," Clint cut in. "And those two directed me to a man named Meyer. He didn't tell me much of anything."

Nodding, Rick watched Clint closely. His eyes seemed to peer right through him with a familiarity borne of many years of friendship. "But you found out plenty, I'd wager."

"A bit. First off, I learned that Meyer is the man who handles all of Castiglione's affairs."

"And second?"

"Second, I figured out that Meyer likes Castiglione about as much as you do. Maybe less."

"Really? Then why's he working for him?"

Clint shrugged. "Could be a lot of things. Maybe he's being forced. Maybe he just took the job and got in too far before he realized where it was going. He could also be pulling one over on me."

Rick shook his head. "I doubt that."

"Nobody's perfect. Besides, he is a lawyer and that makes him more dangerous than a cardsharp."

"I hear that," Rick said with a hearty laugh. "Damn, I hate lawyers."

Clint thought back to the look that had been in Meyer's

eyes just before he'd left the office. There was something there that reminded him of a coyote with its leg caught in a trap. On any normal day, that coyote would be shot for running off with a farmer's hen. Killing it would be completely justified.

But this wasn't just any day and at the moment, that coyote wasn't harming anyone. It was just doing what it does. In fact, in both instances, the coyote was the one in trouble. As bad and wily as that coyote could be, it still deserved compassion in desperate times.

"I don't know about that," Clint said. "He wasn't so bad."

Hartman grunted and shook his head. Although he didn't seem convinced, he wasn't about to argue the point either. "Well, whatever you might say about that lawyer, it don't make what Castiglione is doing any better. I'll bet there's plenty more dirt to be dug up on him. My guess is that most of that dirt is right here in Labyrinth."

"That's my guess too. And I mean to keep digging."

For a few moments, both men leaned back and soaked up the atmosphere. Places like saloons had lives of their own. There was no question why plenty of folks liked to spend their nights in saloons. Anyone who had to ask about it had never been in one.

There was an energy that crackled through the air, which always reminded Clint of sitting just beneath a waterfall. It flowed through him, cleansing him and drenching him to the bone at the same time. There was good and bad, depending on how the water flowed that day.

This time, it was definitely good. People were having a good time and there was enough laughter to bring a smile to both men's faces. The girls strutted around, looking their way and spreading their own kind of joy throughout the place. To top if off, someone was bringing two plates of piping hot food to their table.

"You know something?" Rick said. "Every now and then I feel like a king in this place."

Clint nodded. "I can see why. Feels like a good night."

"It sure is. Every now and then it gets hard to pay for it all, but in the end it's worth it." Picking up his knife and fork, Hartman clenched a fist around the silverware instead of simply holding it. His face had taken on an intensity as well. "That's why I can't bear the thought of someone like Paul Castiglione coming around here and trying to carve off a piece of this for himself.

"There have been plenty of tough-talking bad men coming through here trying to steal something or other, but I can usually drive them off. Castiglione ain't like that. What he's got is legal and there's not a damn thing I can do about it!" Rick punctuated that last sentiment by pounding his fists on the table. By the look on his face, even he was surprised at his vehemence.

"That's what friends are for, Rick," Clint assured him.

"But I don't want this to get violent. I don't want my friends getting hurt. That's why I was hoping to keep you out of it."

"Well, it's too late for that. Besides, you're not the only one involved. There's other businessmen out there getting hurt worse than you. And if you want to handle some things on your own, don't worry about that. When the time comes, you'll have plenty to do. We both will."

FOURTEEN

Once business was out of the way, Clint sat back and enjoyed his meal with Rick. The two friends always had plenty of stories to swap and this was no exception. No matter what else was hanging over their heads, it was important to savor the good times. Any man who lived by the gun knew that much for certain.

The music got loud, the food wasn't bad, and the jokes were. By the time it was over, the sky was black as pitch and the wind was howling outside. It was a wild Texas wind that blew in all the way from the desert like a wraith that had lost all its mercy during the trip. It rattled shutters against windows and knocked dust up against the entire town. But that wasn't anything new to anyone. It just made it seem all the better to be inside.

Another good thing about that wild wind was that it provided excellent cover for anyone who knew how to use it. It just so happened that Clint was one such person.

With a bandanna tied tightly around his mouth and nose, Clint used one hand to hold on to his hat while the other stayed close to his gun. He was going by Rick Hartman's directions, which soon took him into enemy territory. The

building was on the edge of town and still bore the sign of
a mining company that had long ago gone under.

According to Rick, that old mining company was now
being used by Paul Castiglione as a sort of headquarters
for his business in Labyrinth. Since Clint wanted to deal
with Castiglione without shedding too much blood, he
needed to find out a bit more about the man and his business. It required a bit of sneaking about during foul
weather, but it was a price Clint was willing to pay.

Unfortunately, even he didn't think it would be enough.
Men like Castiglione seemed to thrive on shedding blood,
even if it turned out to be their own.

Normally, Clint preferred to keep his steps quiet and his
body in the shadows when he was trying to prowl around
unnoticed. This time, however, the Texas wind was provid-
ing all the cover he could ask for. A dust storm had blown
in from the south and was sending enough grit into the air
to make seeing anything beyond a few feet in front of you
damn near impossible.

Shadows didn't matter since every bit of space was either walled off or filled with sand and dirt. Stepping softly
wasn't even a concern since the steady wind howled like
something from a nightmare as it rolled through town,
scratching along every board and pane of glass in the process. Clint walked with normal steps, albeit somewhat
slower just to make sure he didn't walk straight into something hidden by the dust. In fact, he even stepped a little
heavier just so he could hear himself every now and then.

The combination of the late hour and raging winds
made Clint damn near invisible. He made his way down
the familiar streets until he finally got to the place that Paul
Castiglione called home. The building was right where
Rick said it would be and even had the battered sign to
mark it.

Even though he was knowledgeable of his surroundings

and how to conduct himself within the dust storm, Clint still almost walked straight into an armed man posted not too far from the building's entrance. Clint froze in his tracks the instant he picked the man out of the swirling chaos around him.

Unfortunately, Clint didn't stop until he was only about five feet in front of him.

Clint couldn't make out the man's face, since the guard was wearing a bandanna as well. But Clint did have his instincts to guide him and waited until those instincts screamed at him before making another move.

The guard narrowed his eyes and squinted through a particularly bad gust of wind. He tried focusing on the shape he'd seen a moment ago, but that shape was gone. Now, there were just more shadows in its place. It was as though the figure he'd seen had been made of sand itself and had since been blown away.

Having already put the guard behind him, Clint moved around the building until he was standing at one of the front corners. He stopped there when he heard what sounded like two big pieces of wood being crunched beneath a wheel. That sound was actually just the door being forced open against the wind and grit that had collected on the ground.

Clint could tell by the reluctant way the figure walked as he came outside, as well as the bandanna around his face, that he was probably about to spell the other guard for the night. Before the replacement could get too far, Clint rushed up behind him.

Since the other man turned and looked a second before Clint got there, it seemed that Clint's steps weren't as quiet as he'd thought.

FIFTEEN

The other man started to say something, but it came out as just a muffled grumble from behind his bandanna. Even if he could have understood it, Clint wouldn't have paid it any mind. He was too busy trying to overtake the other man before he got to where he was going.

Acting purely on instinct, the other man reached for the gun at his side as Clint came upon him like another part of the storm. Just as his hand found the grip of his pistol, the man felt something lock down on top of that same hand. While he might have a hold on his weapon, he wasn't able to lift the thing from its holster.

Clint made sure that the other man's hand stayed right where it was. He could have drawn his own gun, but it wasn't the time for that. For the moment, all Clint wanted was to keep a shot from getting fired or more noise from getting made. It was a noble intention, but it also turned out to be the shortest road to catching a swift punch in the face.

Clint started to turn away from the punch, but the storm kept him from seeing that fist until it was too late. The punch caught him on the jaw, but was a glancing blow. Even so, it rattled him enough to ease his grip upon the pistol he'd been holding in place.

The other man's smile was hidden behind his bandanna, but it was reflected well enough in his eyes. Lifting his gun from its holster, he picked out his first shot at the same time he felt his last meal suddenly welling up at the back of his throat.

It took a moment for the pain to set in, but when it did, it rushed through the man's body like a wave and forced him to suck in a deep breath of dusty air. Clint's fist had pounded into the spot just below the man's solar plexus and stayed there long enough to double him over. Less than a second after the fist was retracted, it came back to pound directly into the same spot one more time.

Clint knew well enough to stand away as the man squatted down and started to teeter on his feet. The guy started to heave and forgot all about drawing his pistol when he grabbed his stomach with both hands. The man opened his mouth and retched painfully into his bandanna.

Judging by the look in the fellow's eyes, it was a toss-up as to what made him sicker: being punched twice in his gut or being forced to swallow his own puke soon afterward.

Whichever it was, Clint had to admit that he felt for the guy. Rather than do any more harm, Clint relieved the fellow of his weapon and led him over to a spot where he could sit down and get his breath back. Of course, he could get his breath back just the same hog-tied with his own belt as he could any other way.

Clint made a slow path around the building and couldn't find another guard patrolling the area. Either that meant there was only the one guard outside or the rest were someplace Clint couldn't see them. Whichever it was, there wasn't much else Clint could do about it.

Before he did anything else, Clint paused and stood just outside of the original guard's field of vision. It seemed that the other man was aware that something was going on. He stood in the blowing dust, looking toward the building expectantly.

Sometimes, it was wisest to take the path of least resistance, so Clint adopted the posture of the other man who'd so recently stepped out of the building. Walking up a few steps closer, Clint stopped when he saw he'd been spotted by the guard.

"Somethin' wrong?" the guard shouted over the gusting wind.

Clint shook his head and shouted back through his bandanna, "Just a bit longer. I'll be right back."

"Goddamnit. I'm starvin'!"

But Clint waved off the other man and turned his back on him just like any good friend would in that same position. Apparently, the guard wasn't too surprised by the snub since he kept the rest of his grumblings to himself and continued patrolling the area around the building.

When he'd first stepped out of Rick's Place and felt the wind kicking up around him, Clint had cursed the unpredictable Texas weather. The storm had come like a bolt from the blue, but it wasn't so extraordinary that it got more than some similar grunts from the locals.

Now, with the dust curling around him and acting as a perfect mask and partial shield, Clint had to tip his hat to the same wind he'd cursed before. Now, the storm was a blessing and it allowed him to walk straight past the guard, past any lookouts Castiglione might have had posted and right up to Paul's front door.

Clint doubted that Paul would find the weather quite so amusing.

SIXTEEN

Paul stood looking out a window, bracing himself with one hand against the wall. Dust pattered against the glass in front of him as he shook his head and scowled at his own reflection. "Jesus H. Christ. Where in the hell did this storm come from?"

"I heard someone say there was one coming. I think it was ol' Willie Sweetwater."

"That old coot? He says there's a twister coming every time his right elbow gets an ache."

"Looks like he was right this time."

The front door came open, but Paul didn't even bother to look at who it was. Instead, he grunted and lifted the shot glass he'd been holding in his other hand. "What the hell do you know about anything, Sam? And why ain't you out there walking the perimeter?"

"Because that's not my job." A few steps sounded through the room as the door slammed and was held shut by the wind. Now that the storm was outside once again, Clint's next words echoed through the room like a whole new tempest. "And I'm not Sam."

Paul didn't even have to turn his head. His eyes were still focused upon the window. This time, he was staring at

64

Clint's reflection instead of his own. "Well, well," he said. "Look what the wind blew in."

There were two others inside the room and there was enough tension in their eyes and posture to make up for the cool way Clint and Paul conducted themselves. One of these men was the biggest man that had been at Rick's Place earlier.

"You want me to toss him out of here?" the big man asked.

Paul shook his head. "Nah, Bull. He's here for a reason. I'm curious to hear what it is. Especially since I was so nice to him and his friend before."

Standing his ground without saying a word, Clint looked around to make sure that he wasn't about to be jumped from another angle. There was no doubting that Bull wanted to tear Clint apart, but it seemed the big man was content to follow orders for the moment. The other man in the room had also been at Rick's Place earlier that day. Of course, it was unlikely that Zack was ever too far from Paul's side.

The only one of the men to move was Paul, and that was so he could turn around and look at Clint straight-on. Paul wore a vaguely amused smile as he crossed his arms and leaned back against the wall. "You got here, Gunsmith. Let's hear what you have to say."

"I just thought I'd hear what all this was about straight from the source," Clint said.

"Folks owe me money," Paul said with a shrug. "I'm collecting it. There's no law against that. It's just business."

"What money?"

"I'm the owner of various properties in town. And it's not just this town, but plenty of others too. The man who owned it before was content to take his payments in dribs and drabs, but not me. I need some cash right now and I'm exercisin' a legal way of gettin' it."

"You can stop trying to convince me that you're working

within the law. I've already seen that much and I'm getting sick of hearing it."

"Well, that's just too bad. Tell you the truth, I was thinking you'd be a little more grateful considering how much slack I cut your friend. He owes me more'n near anybody."

"Slack?" Clint asked. "That's a strange word to use for barging into his saloon and picking a fight."

"Could have been a lot worse," Paul replied evenly. "Believe me." He let those words hang in the air as the wind continued to smack up against the window. "Jesus, this storm is something else. I swear it just came down from out of the blue."

Clint shot back with, "So did these payments of yours."

"I'm actually doing these folks a favor. Once they pay me off, the land they bought is all theirs and the loans they took out are all paid off."

"And what if they aren't able to pay on your schedule?"

"Then their loans are for fretted or . . ." Paul snapped his fingers a few times and glanced over to Zack. "How d'ya say that?"

The little guy was more than happy to oblige by perking up and saying, "Forfeit. The loans are forfeited."

Paul nodded. "That's the word I was looking for. What that means, Adams, is that the land becomes mine and so does whatever's sitting on it. I wasn't looking to branch off into so many businesses, but if that's the way it goes, I'll be glad to take over."

"You said these contracts you acquired cover properties in more than one town," Clint pointed out. "How many more?"

"Nearly half a dozen within a hundred miles," Paul replied. The smile on his face had gone from amused to hungry in the time it had taken for him to draw a breath. "That strike you as a lot?"

Clint shifted his eyes around the room one more time. So far, the others were still staying put. Every so often,

Bull would take a half step closer. Clint caught him in one such movement now and halted him with a stern glare.

"It strikes me as awful peculiar that a man like you just happens to get his hands on such valuable documents," Clint said. "And it's even more peculiar that you knew what the hell to do with them."

Paul straightened up. If he'd had feathers, every one of them would have been ruffled right about now. "What's that supposed to mean, Adams? You sayin' I'm dumb?"

Bull twitched and squared his shoulders as well. This was the very moment he'd been waiting for. Judging by the expectant look on his face, it seemed more likely he'd been praying for this moment to come.

"You're no lawyer, I'll say that much," Clint pointed out. "But dumb? I guess it did take a little bit of brains to figure out this scheme. I guess ignorant is more the word I was after."

Paul looked as though he wanted to be offended. Bull looked the same way, but no matter how much they looked at each other, neither of the gunmen could figure out what that word meant. Although Zack was dying to give an explanation, Paul moved on without it.

"I had some help, but I'm running this show now. What you should be more interested in is that I've got a proposition for you, Adams."

"Oh," Clint said. "This ought to be good."

SEVENTEEN

"It is good," Paul said with confidence. "I need someone more persuasive to talk to these people. You're just the man. You carry a lot of weight around here."

"You want me to be a collector?" Clint asked. "Collecting from my own friends?"

"Yeah."

"And why would I want to do that?"

"Because if you don't, I'll start cutting my losses. You know what that means? It means I start closing down these businesses and clearing off my land any way I choose. Mostly, I think I'll tear the places down and sell the lumber. What do you think?"

As soon as he saw he was in Paul's sight again, Zack started nodding like his head was attached to a spring. "Yeah, that sounds great!"

"It is my le—" Paul cut himself short by placing a quick finger against his mouth. When he took it away again, he said, "It's my right."

"And what's in it for me?" Clint asked, still in disbelief.

"Well, for starters your friends can keep what they got and pay off their debts. I might even move on to one of my favorite places instead of lying around this pisshole of a town any longer. More'n that, there's a mighty big profit in it for you, Adams. Mighty big."

Clint stepped forward as if none of the others in the room were even there. The moment he got too close to Paul, Bull lunged as if he'd been loosed from a tight bowstring. The big man reached out with a massive hand that was meant to close painfully around the back of Clint's neck.

Half a second before Bull's hand got to where it was going, Clint spun on the balls of his feet and batted the hand away with his own wrist. Rather than merely deflect Bull's arm, Clint snaked his own arm around it until he locked the big man up tightly.

Twisting Bull's arm so it was turned the wrong way, Clint locked his eyes on the big man's face as he applied just enough pressure to bring a wince to Bull's face. As much as he tried to muscle his way free, the only thing Bull succeeded in doing was getting himself into even deeper trouble.

"Hurts, doesn't it?" Clint asked as he cinched in his grip. "Your elbow doesn't bend this way, does it?" Now, he could move anywhere he wanted and the only thing Bull could do was go along for the ride.

Bull started to spit a curse at Clint, but was cut short by the slightest movement against his locked elbow. Bull's face flushed and he could feel his elbow was about to snap if Clint made one wrong move in that direction.

"Y . . . yeah," Bull grunted. "It hurts."

Clint nodded and looked up to find Paul and Zack staring back at them. Judging by the look on Zack's face, this was the first time he'd ever seen Bull compromised in the slightest. Paul, on the other hand, managed to keep up appearances a little better.

"Let's get one thing straight," Clint said. "I came here to let you know that, whatever business you've got, you can handle it in a proper manner. Legal or not, all you're doing is pushing these folks around to fill your pockets. You showed your true colors when you came barging into that saloon like a pack of wild dogs."

Paul listened carefully as the muscles in his jaw clenched.

"You offering that job to me was an insult," Clint said. "Plain and simple. I don't work for the likes of you, and I'm not the kind of man to make a living off of stealing contracts from dead bodies and sifting through them for loopholes."

Although he still looked pissed as hell, Paul didn't flinch when he heard Clint say that.

"So figure out a respectable arrangement and propose it to the people you've been trying to rob," Clint continued. "That's the legal way to conduct yourself. And keep your pets on a leash, for Christ's sake."

With that, Clint released Bull's arm and shoved the bigger man away from him. He waited for Bull to wheel around and come at him, bracing himself for the worst.

Although Bull did exactly as Clint had expected, he stopped short once again before following through. His blood was pumping so fast through his veins that his chest was heaving like a bellows. His hands curled into fists, ignoring the gun at his side. All Bull had to do was take a quick peek toward Paul to know what his orders would be.

And all Paul had to do was lift a hand at the proper moment to relay those orders.

"Good," Clint said as he saw all that was going on around him. "Glad to see that things don't have to get too ugly."

"You want ugly, Adams?" Paul asked. "You'll see plenty of ugly before this is through. I promise you, if I'm not allowed to go about my own business, I'll make this uglier than you could even imagine."

"I wouldn't say that too quickly. I can imagine quite a bit."

There was something else in Clint's words that lay just beneath them the way a viper lay and waited for its prey in the grass. That same deadly promise could be seen in Clint's eyes and since Paul didn't have any more tough words to say, it seemed that he saw it just fine.

"West Texas is a big place," Clint said as he headed toward the door. "And Labyrinth is a great town. You shouldn't have any trouble finding a better way to earn your money."

Clint pulled open the door and moved outside. Every step he took was careful and every muscle in his body was prepared to answer any threat that might come his way.

"No, Bull," Paul said after a single heavy step was taken. "Let him go."

The storm was still raging as Clint left, and it swallowed him up after he took a few steps into the night. The door slammed shut, leaving Paul and his men alone to contemplate the meeting they'd just had.

A few moments later, the door was pulled open. Paul and Bull turned and drew their guns as they got a look at who'd opened the door. Their fingers were about to pull their triggers before they even got a look at the familiar face poking in from the storm.

"Hey, fellas," Sam said as he tugged his bandanna down and glanced nervously at the steel in the others' hands. "Is someone gonna take my place out there or not? I'm starving."

EIGHTEEN

Two days after the dust storm blew through Labyrinth, the only thing occupying the locals' time was clearing away the dirt. Accustomed to such storms, folks in town merely swept their porches and cleaned their clothes until the storm was just another topic of conversation.

There was a bigger storm brewing, however. The only difference with this one was that not all folks knew it was coming. Although there was most definitely tension in the air, it wasn't the sort of thing that many people could pin down. Even a farmer's sensitive joints were no help in detecting the tempest on the horizon.

Clint and Rick, on the other hand, knew all too well what was on its way. The only question that remained in their mind was when it would arrive.

One good thing about the dust storm that had dropped in on Labyrinth from out of nowhere was that it left the skies overhead clear and blue. Clint sat in a chair outside of Rick's Place and leaned back so he could rest his feet up on a wooden rail. He folded his hands across his belly and pulled in a large, clean breath. The fresh air swirled around inside of him like cool water. When he let it out, he felt all the better for it.

"You look like the cat that just swallowed the canary," Rick said as he stepped outside and pulled up a chair beside Clint. "You been seeing that stable girl again?"

Clint glanced over at his friend and gave him a half scowl. "How'd you know about that?"

"Women talk, Clint. And barkeeps listen. That's pretty much the same wherever you go."

Shaking his head, Clint looked back to the sky and said, "I may have seen her once or twice."

"Is that what's got you so happy?"

"Can't a fellow relax and enjoy a pleasant day without having to answer for it?"

Rick shrugged, leaned back, and looked at the same patch of sky that Clint was so focused upon. Finally, he muttered, "The day is pretty nice. That storm was foul, but it seemed to have taken all the rest of the clouds with it. Kind of like ol' Mother Nature gave us her best shot and took a rest."

"You always did have a way with words, Rick."

"Yeah, and I taught you a thing or two about reading people. How many times have I soaked you for all you had at cards?"

"Enough that thinking about it too long might just spoil my good mood."

"Then you should know better than to try keeping things from me." Waiting for a local to step around their chairs and move on, Rick lowered his voice and said, "It's a nice day, but not that nice. You haven't said a damn thing about what happened between you and Castiglione. Now, you look like you just got dealt a royal flush. What's up?"

Clint kept quiet for a little while longer, but only to wait until Rick seemed like he was about to bust. He knew better than to try and keep anything from his friend. Rick hadn't been kidding about teaching him more than a few lessons on reading people. Finally, Clint broke the silence when he looked over to Rick's anxious face.

"Have you seen hide or hair of Paul or his men lately?"

Rick scowled first, but then took a moment to think it over. When he looked back to Clint, Rick's scowl was gone. "Come to think of it, I haven't."

"Why do you think that is?"

"Did you scare them off?"

Although he paused for a moment, Clint shook his head. "I doubt that, but I do think he's moved on to some other town for the time being."

"All right. Tell me what's on yer mind."

Clint took a few moments to spell out everything that had happened and everything that had been said during his last visit with Castiglione. Since there was still the occasional passerby, Clint left out some of the more colorful details, but told Rick about all the important facts he'd discovered. When he was finished, Clint saw an appreciative smirk on Hartman's face.

"I knew there was more you weren't telling me," Rick said. "Sure took you long enough to tell me about it."

"I wanted to hold off just in case Castiglione or some of his boys did some poking around of their own. It would be better for you to not know anything at all if that happened."

"Guess I can't fault you for that. Still, that don't make hearing it any easier." He paused for a moment before glancing back over at Clint. "You know he'll be back, right? I mean, if he fancies himself such a businessman, he'll be back to collect his fees."

"Yeah. I know."

After studying his friend a bit more, Rick said, "You don't owe me a thing, you know. If you've got things to do, you can head out of here whenever you like."

"I know."

"But somehow I get the feeling that wasn't what you had in mind."

"No," Clint said. "It wasn't."

"Mind filling me in?"

"You want my opinion?"

"No, but that's never stopped you from giving it before," Rick said with a wry grin.

"I think you and these other men Paul's been after are too close to this. I've seen it before. When there's too much at stake for a man, it becomes all too easy for him too move too far or too fast."

"I can handle myself, Clint. You know that."

"I know and I wouldn't say otherwise. After seeing how Castiglione and his men operate, I also know that taking one wrong step against him could be a big mistake. He's ready to draw blood," Clint said in a more serious tone. "All of those men are. That's why I've been staying around here to make sure that there weren't any repercussions on their way."

"Well, you said that they packed up and moved along."

"True, but not for good. They'll be back. Actually, I think he's just gone to check in on some of his other investments while hoping I won't be here when he gets back."

"After what you pulled a few nights ago," Rick said, "that sounds about right."

"Well, since you and the rest of the men involved in this have so much at stake, that means someone outside of the situation would have a much better shot at clearing this up."

"Always ready to come riding in to the rescue, aren't you?" Rick mused. "Maybe we should just leave this to the law."

"You know that's useless. If Castiglione has done anything right, it's been covering his backside legally."

"So that leaves just you?" Rick shook his head. "I don't like the thought of you risking yourself for something like this."

"I don't mind taking a risk for the right cause. And if a man can't risk himself for a friend, what other cause should he choose?"

There was a moment that passed between Rick and Clint that didn't need words. Rick's eyes showed a gratitude that was expressed well enough by the smile that drifted onto his face.

"So what's your first move?" Rick asked. "Or do I even want to know?"

"First, I need to let Castiglione know that just because the dust has settled, that doesn't mean the storm has passed. Wherever he is, there's going to be a whirlwind. I'll see to it myself."

NINETEEN

Half of any good plan was in knowing when to set it into motion. If going against the odds for so many years had taught Clint anything, that was one of the biggest lessons.

Although he'd done a good enough job in besting Castiglione on his home turf once, Clint didn't want to push his luck a second time until the time was right. There were too many other things at stake, ranging from the livelihood of several good folks in Labyrinth to the very lives of those same people as well as those of anyone else who happened to get in the way.

Clint had bided his time for a few days until he was certain that Castiglione had gone to check on some of his other interests. Now, the next thing on Clint's list was to figure out where those other interests might actually be.

No matter what he thought about lawyers, even Clint had to admit that they were good for one or two things. First on that list was keeping records. If Harold Meyer truly was representing Castiglione in some fashion, and Clint was sure that he was, then Meyer would have to know some things about his client. And some things to lawyers meant a whole lot of mind-numbing details to most everyone else.

It was getting into the dark hours of the day, but with the sky so clear, it seemed that the sunlight just didn't want to go away. That was fine to Clint since he wasn't in any particular need of heavy cover at the moment. In fact, the clear, velvety sky and the glittering gems scattered overhead might just work to his advantage.

Keeping his steps light and casual, Clint made his way down the street and nodded to the dwindling number of other folks heading down that same boardwalk. By the time he reached the building holding Meyer's office, Clint was practically alone. He was alone, that is, until he opened the door and stepped inside.

There was just enough wind to rustle some of the papers on Kara's desk, which kept the pretty brunette occupied for a moment as she quickly tried to keep them from flying away. She was dressed in a simple yellow dress and the ribbon tied around her throat was dark brown. Her hair was tied in a single tail that allowed more of her face to be seen.

"We're about to close," she said in a vaguely annoyed tone without looking up from the papers that were about to spill off of her desk. "And besides that, Mr. Meyer has already left for the day."

"That's a shame," Clint said as he removed his hat and rushed forward to catch a paper that was just about to slip through her fingers. "But seeing a sight as pretty as you makes it awfully hard to get upset about it."

Kara's eyes snapped up and it was plain to see that she'd already recognized Clint's voice. Even so, she still looked surprised when she saw his smiling face looking down at her. "Oh, it's you, Mr. Adams. I didn't know you'd be stopping by."

"I know. Do I still need an appointment?"

"Well, not as such. Like I said, Mr. Meyer is already gone for the day."

"What about to see you?"

Although that question wasn't expected, the smile that

came to Kara's face made it clear that she wasn't entirely blindsided by it either. "I'm more than happy to see you, Mr. Adams. What can I do for you?"

"First of all, call me Clint."

She shuffled the papers until they were once again in a neat, symmetrical stack. "All right. What can I do for you, Clint?"

"I was wondering if I might be able to get a look at some records."

Her eyes narrowed a bit as Kara seemed to study Clint a little closer. "What records are you talking about?"

Sitting on the edge of her desk, Clint said, "The records concerning Mr. Castiglione's interests. Not all of the records. I would just like to see how many there are and where they might be."

Kara arched her eyebrow and started to laugh under her breath. "Oh, that's not too much."

Although Clint smiled expectantly, he didn't truly expect her to budge an inch. Unfortunately, his skill at reading other people was still alive and well.

"I can't let you see any records," Kara said. "You must know that."

"How long have you lived here?"

She was put off by the sudden change in subject, but adjusted well enough to reply, "A few years."

"That's long enough to get to know the people that live here."

"Yes, but—"

"And have you met Paul Castiglione?"

Letting out a breath, Kara nodded. "Yes. A few times."

"Do you have any idea what he's been doing to some of the honest people in Labyrinth?"

Although she tried to maintain the edge in her voice, she nodded and said, "Yes, Clint. I do." Her voice had taken on a new tone, one that indicated that she might have even known more than Clint had originally guessed.

"Knowing all that, you must know that Castiglione isn't exactly the most honest of Meyer's clients."

Kara didn't say anything to that right away. In fact, she didn't have to say a word. The way she cast her eyes downward and pulled in a deep breath spoke volumes.

"I can't let you just poke around in Mr. Meyer's office," she told him.

Clint shook his head. "Of course not. I was kind of hoping for a sort of guided tour." Although he saw that her original smile was returning, Clint was quick to add, "All I need to know is how far Castiglione's reach is. Any details beyond names and locations of a few of the bigger businesses can be kept well away from me."

"And I suppose you'd like me to give you this tour myself?"

Holding out his hand, Clint said, "Well, there's no time like the present."

TWENTY

Not only did Kara take Clint's hand, but she held on to it from the time that she stood up from her desk all the way until they were approaching Meyer's door. Halfway down the hall, Clint realized that she was doing this more as a way to keep track of his whereabouts than simply show her affection.

That didn't mean the walk was all business, however. Every so often, she would glance over her shoulder. When she saw that Clint was watching her intently, Kara would give him a smile that had nothing at all to do with business.

From Clint's perspective, keeping his mind on the task at hand was becoming more and more difficult with every step. The deep yellow dress that Kara wore clung to her hips nicely, accentuating every movement of her firm little buttocks. The long black tail of hair that was tied behind her head swung like a cat's tail, further distracting Clint.

"Just one moment," she whispered. "I'll unlock the door."

Despite the slow way that she'd led him to the door, Kara was quick about getting it open for them. She found the key without a hitch, fitted it into the lock and soon the door was swinging open for both of them to enter. She

stepped inside and held it open so she could close it up
again as soon as Clint had entered.

"Careful about any lights in here," she whispered. "Mr.
Meyer doesn't live too far from here and I swear he
watches this place when he eats his supper."

"Likes to take his work home, does he?"

Rolling her eyes, Kara nodded. "It's all he thinks about."

"Well," Clint said as he shifted his eyes to the lawyer's
desk and the cabinets surrounding it, "let's just hope he
doesn't take all of it home with him."

Kara was singling out another key from the small ring
she'd fished from her pocket. "Here, let me try to make this
a little easier." She walked straight toward one of the
smaller, more solidly built cabinets beside Meyer's desk.
"I'm pretty sure he would keep papers like the ones you're
after in here."

"I really appreciate this."

"Just remember," she said while rifling through a stack
of folded documents, "You only get to look at what I show
you. Any more than that and I'll make sure the sheriff
hears about it."

"Don't worry about me. I'm sure whatever you show me
will be just fine."

Kara picked up on the suggestion in his voice and
smiled to herself. Her fingers quickened as they moved
from one paper to another and her heartbeat picked up a
little within her breast.

"Here you go," she said once she'd located a particular
document and given it a quick once-over. "This must be
what you're after."

Clint made sure that his eyes were looking at her face by
the time she turned around. He was pleasantly surprised to
see that she was handing over a fairly thick stack of documents rather than the one or two sheets he'd been expecting.

He reached over for a lantern and looked back to her before turning the knob. "May I?"

"All right," she said reluctantly. "Just be careful. Remember . . ." Rather than finish the sentence, she winced and pointed toward the window behind Meyer's desk. Even though the shades were drawn, they were thin enough that the paltry light coming from the outside was already starting to show through them.

Clint put the lantern on the cabinet and stood so his body was between it and the window. That way, when he twisted the knob slowly, his shadow fell over the window rather than anything that might attract outside attention.

When he looked over to Kara, Clint found an approving smile on her face. That smile didn't fade when he started studying the papers he'd given her and flipping on down through the stack.

"You wouldn't happen to have a piece of paper and a pencil for me, would you?" Clint asked.

Kara disappeared from his sight for a moment and came back with the items he'd requested. The moment she handed them over, Clint started scribbling notes down onto the paper. Between flipping through the documents and taking his notes, Clint's hands barely stopped moving and his eyes hardly strayed from the poorly lit pages.

"This is a big help," Clint said. Pausing for a moment, he glanced up at her and added, "You didn't have to do this, you know."

She nodded. "I know."

He flipped the page, nodded and said, "Actually, this is a whole lot more than I was after. I'm truly indebted to you."

"My uncle is part owner of Mason's Dry Goods. It's a store that just opened a few months ago. Just in time for Castiglione to start demanding his payments. The way things are going, my uncle and his partner will be broke in a few weeks. You want to pay me back?" she asked. "Then use this information however you want, just so long as it hurts Paul Castiglione."

Clint had just flipped over a paper that mentioned Mason's Dry Goods. It wasn't the source of much income, but it wasn't a very big business either. Small or large, it was a crippling blow to any business if the land got pulled out from under it.

After another minute or two of frantic scribbling, Clint handed the pencil back to Kara and folded up his paper so it would fit in his pocket. There was plenty more information to be had from what he'd been shown, but all of the important parts were copied down.

"I've got more than enough here to do some damage," Clint said, patting his pocket.

"Good."

"I guess we should get going before anyone notices the desk downstairs is empty."

"Actually," Kara said, barring Clint's way with a quickly outstretched arm, "there was another reason I brought you up here."

Clint smiled and let himself drift close enough for their breaths to brush over each other's lips. He kissed her gently at first, but then felt Kara respond strongly to the advance.

"Good." Clint breathed. "I was hoping we were thinking along the same lines."

TWENTY-ONE

Kara's lips tasted vaguely sweet and spicy at the same time. Part of that might have come from the excitement flowing through her, but the rest of it came naturally from her own self. When they kissed a second time, their hands became busy, running up and down each other's bodies until they started snagging upon various articles of clothing.

Once a piece of clothing became too much of a hindrance, it was immediately pulled open or pushed to one side. Either way, they both started to get fleeting touches of bare skin against their fingers. From there, the burning embers inside of them truly started to heat up.

Smiling at Clint, Kara leaned back against the cabinet and let her own hands move slowly along the front of her dress. One by one, she unfastened the buttons, slowly revealing the more delicate undergarments made of thin cotton and edged in lace.

Clint didn't take his eyes off of her for a moment. In fact, he stepped back so he could get an even better view of her as she slowly peeled the dress down over her shoulders. The firm, rounded curves of her breasts were highlighted in the dim, flickering light of the lantern. With the shadows jumping across her body and her hands moving along

85

those supple curves, her nipples quickly became erect and poked up from beneath the slip.

As Clint moved toward her again, he could feel her hands busily pulling at his belt. The more she worked to undress him, the more desperate she became to get her hands on his bare flesh. When she finally was able to slip her hands down between his legs, Kara let out a sigh that matched Clint's own.

Her slender fingers easily found the thick shaft of his penis, wrapped around it, and started stroking in slow, easy motions. She did that until he was firm and rigid in her grasp. Kara's eyes grew wide when she realized that she couldn't get her arm down the front of his pants far enough to stroke his entire length.

That little problem was solved quickly enough. Using both hands, Kara stripped Clint from the waist down. Rather than let her do all the work, Clint pulled her slip up until it was bunched around her waist. His other hand began massaging her hip and thigh before slipping between her legs to gently rub the moist lips of her vagina.

"Oh God," Kara whispered. Soon, her eyes drifted toward the wall behind Clint's back as well as the looming shadow he was projecting onto it. "Oh God." This time, when she said those words, there was something else in her voice that made Clint pause in what he was doing.

Clint looked up from where his face had been buried in the crook of Kara's neck and turned to look in the direction that she was looking. At first, he didn't see anything but a shadow on the wall. Soon, he was able to make out the shape, which was clearly his hand working along a smooth, definitely feminine, curve.

Quickly, Clint reached out to snuff out the light coming from the lantern. After that, there was only the dim light from the sky to spill in on them after making its way through the blinds. Already, the room felt cooler and more

intimate. Clint hardly noticed since he'd quickly gone back
to what he'd been doing before the distraction.

He savored feeling every inch of her naked skin. Since
he had to push up her slip to get to her, touching Kara's
body felt like a sort of prize that he was winning every moment. She was still touching him as well, stroking his erection until he felt like he was about to explode.

Taking a deep breath, Clint moved in closer while lifting Kara up into his arms. Her legs wrapped around him
and she arched her back against the cabinet behind her.
Just as she felt her shoulders bump against the wooden
structure, she felt Clint's rigid cock press against the wet
folds of her pussy.

As he pushed his hips forward, Kara thrust hers out until every inch of his erection was enveloped by her soft,
smooth lips. For a while, both of them let the seconds pass
through them. They enjoyed the feel of each other as well
as the perfect intimacy of the moment. Finally, Clint
started pushing in and out of her until Kara's breaths built
into a passionate groan.

Clint's hands cupped her tight buttocks, holding her up
against the cabinet as he pumped between her legs. He
barely even noticed her weight. Instead, he focused on the
warmth of her body pressed against his and the way every
muscle under her skin writhed and wriggled against him.

Kara's eyes were closed and her face was turned to one
side. One arm was wrapped around the back of Clint's
neck while the other slid up and down along the side of the
cabinet. By the look on her face, it seemed that she was enjoying a particularly good dream. Every now and then, her
lips would part and a contented sigh would slip out from
the back of her throat.

Suddenly, there was a noise coming from outside the
door. Clint froze and Kara lowered her feet to the floor.
Neither one of them moved a muscle until they heard the

patter of small feet along the floor followed by the soft mew of a cat.

"That'd be Pepper," Kara said with a grin. "My kitten."

Clint smirked and let his eyes drift down her body. Kara's slip clung to her flesh, granting him enough of a view of what was underneath to make him start to ache for her once again. As if sensing this from him, Kara stepped away from the cabinet until she got to the middle of the room.

From there, she turned her back to Clint and placed her hands against the edge of the desk. Kara arched her back until her perfect little backside completed the delicious curve of her spine. Her black hair was still tied behind her head, but now fell over her shoulders in strands.

Already, Clint was moving up behind her. He placed his hands on her hips and took a moment to rub them. From there, he inched forward again until the tip of his cock was rubbing along the smooth curve of her buttocks.

"Oh Clint," she whispered. "Don't make me wait any longer. I don't think I can take it."

"You're not the only one."

The moment she felt Clint's rigid penis slip between her legs, Kara lowered her head and widened her stance a bit more to accommodate him. She gripped the edge of the desk and pulled in a slow breath in anticipation of what was to come. In the next moment, she felt him enter her once again and slowly fill her until his hips were pressed against her backside.

Kara's low, throaty moan filled the entire room.

Clint looked down to let his eyes trace the line that started at the nape of her neck and ran all the way down to where her body met his. Her back arched and her muscles tensed every time he pushed inside of her. As he picked up his rhythm, Clint felt her start to move with him.

Soon, Clint was gripping her hips tightly so he could pound into her with building force. Before too long, the desk was rattling beneath her and Kara was holding on to it so tightly that she nearly pushed it against the wall. This time, she was the one who nearly announced what was happening in the office by crying out so loudly that she would have been heard on the street outside.

Before she made a sound, Kara bit down on her lower lip and struggled through until the moment passed. The moment that followed was just as big of a test, however, since an orgasm was building up inside of her that threatened to rock her like an explosion.

One more powerful thrust was all it took. Truth be told, neither one of them knew how they managed to keep from crying out. In fact, neither one of them knew how they managed to not spend the entire night locked away in that office.

TWENTY-TWO

"Did you get everything you were after?"

The question came at Clint from the saloon's owner the moment he walked into Rick's Place. Although he knew exactly what Rick meant, the last thing that came to Clint's mind just then was anything to do with Castiglione.

"And then some," was Clint's reply. Even though it fit what was going through his mind, it was also applicable to what both men were thinking.

Rick nodded and smiled broadly. "Good, good. How'd you manage to pull it off? Did you have to sweet talk your way past someone in the office?"

"That doesn't matter," Clint said. "All that does matter is that I got what I needed. In fact, I got even more information than I'd hoped." He took out the folded paper from his pocket and held it out for Rick to see. "With what I've got written down here, I should be able to do plenty."

Despite the anxiousness that was written all over his face, Rick kept himself from saying another word. Instead, he motioned for Clint to come closer to the bar. Only once Clint was close enough to hear him when he lowered his voice, did Rick bother saying anything else.

"No need to let anyone else know what we're up to," Hartman said. "Never know who's listening."

Clint looked around at the dozen or so locals who were scattered throughout the saloon. Not one of them seemed to have taken more than a passing notice of Clint's arrival, but Clint still respected Rick's need to be cautious.

"Here," Clint said as he placed the paper flat upon the top of the bar and turned it around so Rick could read it. "Take a look at this." Tapping his finger against something he'd written, Clint asked, "Does that mean anything to you?"

Rick squinted down at the notes and nodded. "Those numbers you wrote down next to the name of my place," he said. "That's how much I've paid him over the last few months."

"And these dates?" Clint asked.

"That's when I made the payments. I kept track of them myself, so that's how I'm so certain."

Clint nodded. "Good."

"Is it?"

"It sure is." Clint flipped to another section of the notes he'd taken and pointed them out to Rick. "Take a look here."

Rick squinted down at the paper, took a deep breath and squinted a little harder. He looked a little embarrassed when he glanced over to Clint. Before his friend could say anything, Rick snatched the paper from his hand and held it to within a few inches of his face. "Not a damn word," he grumbled.

Clint watched in amusement and couldn't help himself from saying, "I think you need to get yourself some spectacles."

"What did I just say? That was a lot more than a damn word."

"Sorry," Clint said as he leaned back. Even so, it was impossible to keep the grin from his face.

"Looks like whoever this is, they're not getting hit half as bad as we are," Rick said.

"Take a closer look."

Rick shot a look over to Clint that made it seem as though he were a breath away from giving him a backhand. But Clint nodded to let him know that he wasn't just joshing him some more about his eyesight. Seeing that, Rick did take a closer look.

A second later, Rick's head snapped back a bit in surprise. "I'll be damned! These figures are from Cali Station. That town's the size of this one, easy. Maybe even a little bigger."

"That's right," Clint said.

"That don't make much sense. If Castiglione has interests there, he should be able to soak these fellas for as much as he's soaking us. Hell, he might even be able to get some more out of them."

"Take a closer look."

Rick shook his head at the way Clint repeated himself, but didn't hesitate to follow his direction. He scowled at the paper with such intensity that it wouldn't have been surprising if smoke had started curling off the edges of the page. Finally, Rick started shaking his head even harder and then dropped the paper altogether.

"I don't know what I'm looking for, Clint."

Patiently, Clint reached out to tap his finger on one edge of the notes. "These dates. Check the dates."

Rick took another look, this time focusing on the section that Clint had pointed out. Just as the frustration was starting to creep into his eyes once more, it started to recede. Smiling, he looked back up at Clint and said, "Are these dates when this money was collected?"

Clint smiled as well and nodded. "As far as I can tell."

"Well, that means it's been at least six or seven weeks since Paul's been out that way."

"And how long has he been a burr under your saddle?"

"About a month," Rick replied. "What about the rest of the places you got marked down here?"

"That's the biggest one that's been left alone the longest. There's a few other towns that have gone longer since the last collection, but they're chicken feed compared to what he would get here or at Cali Station."

"And," Rick added as he studied the notes even closer, "those smaller places aren't too far off the trail between here and Cali."

Clint took another quick look himself and then nodded. "I hadn't seen that. But that just makes me more certain I'm right."

"Paul ain't here, so he probably went to Cali Station," Rick said. "The damn coward's probably hoping you won't be here by the time he decides to head this way again so he can pick up where he left off."

"Well, he's got part of that right at least. I'm not going to be here."

Rick smiled widely. "I just wish I could see the look on his face when you get there. That's gonna be priceless."

TWENTY-THREE

Clint had his things packed and ready to go in a matter of minutes after leaving Rick's Place. In fact, now that he knew where to go next, he was more than a little anxious to get on his way. When going up against someone, there were always two definite paths to take.

The first was the most direct and also the bloodiest. Clint could have ended all of Labyrinth's problems by putting a bullet through Paul Castiglione and each of his men. But in Clint's mind, that wasn't even an option—until that was the only option available.

Since he did have some reservations about wholesale slaughter, that left Clint with the second path. That second path took a bit more time, but involved outthinking Castiglione. In Clint's eyes, this path was the most rewarding.

Any man could learn to draw quickly and send enough lead into the air to do some damage. It took real talent to outmaneuver someone and beat him at his own game. The risks were still just as high, but if everything happened the way he wanted, Clint was looking at a much better outcome. If Castiglione was killed, that just left the door open for someone else to walk in and try to take his place.

If Castiglione was taken down and taken apart, there wouldn't be anyone who would want to fill his shoes.

Thinking about this brought a smirk to Clint's face. He had a definite edge here since Castiglione had no way of knowing about the information that Clint had gotten his hands on. A man like Paul surely had some boys hanging around acting as Castiglione's eyes and ears, but more than likely those eyes and ears were scattered throughout the area.

Clint didn't need to go tracking Paul down. He didn't need to ask around and try to find out where he might be. Clint had a real good hunch as to Paul's exact location, which meant he could cut straight through and bypass a good number of Paul's scouts.

Of course, there was always the chance that Clint was giving Paul too much credit. Then again, precautions like that were like being weighed down by full canteens when riding through the desert. It was always better to be too ready than not ready enough.

With that in mind, Clint found himself at Doc Hennessey's office. He knocked on the door and watched as the little veterinarian found his way to it and opened it.

Before Hennessey could greet him, Clint asked, "Is Eclipse still doing well?"

"As well as can be expected. Actually, he's doing even better than—"

"Great," Clint interrupted. "That's just what I wanted to hear." He then took a folded wad of money and tucked it into the doctor's shirt pocket. "There's a little something extra in there for any other expenses you might have incurred. Keep whatever's left over. You certainly earned it."

Hennessey removed the money from his pocket and unfolded it. By the time he got a handle on how much was actually there, he started to sputter and look up excitedly for Clint. But Clint was no longer there. In fact, all Hennessey could see of him was an outline walking toward the nearby stables.

"Thank you, Mr. Adams," Hennessey said. He'd wanted to refuse some of the extra money, but could tell by the purpose in Clint's steps that it would just have been a waste of time. The doctor had looked into enough gift horse's mouths to know better than to look back into this one.

Clint made it into the stables and could hear Eclipse fussing in his stall. Somehow, the Darley Arabian always knew when Clint was ready to go. Either that, or the stallion had been rearing to go himself the entire time. Considering how Eclipse had bolted the last time Clint had ridden him, that second possibility was just as likely.

"Hello?" Clint said into the air. "Anyone here?"

He had another bit of money in his pocket intended to settle up for what was due for use of the livery. All he needed now was someone to give it to.

A heartbeat before Clint could call out again, he heard someone moving next to the door through which he'd just come. He turned quickly to see who it was and found Maggie standing there partially in the shadows.

"There you are," he said. "I wish I had more time, but I just came by to give you th—"

He was cut off by a sudden intensity that burned in her eyes more than anything else. Clint started looking around himself, but got back to her after coming up short. When he saw Maggie's face again, she looked like she was just about to scream.

The footsteps rushing up on Clint from behind told him the rest.

TWENTY-FOUR

Clint turned so that his eyes were the first thing to swing around toward the approaching footsteps. While there was still a chance that there was no danger, that possibility was getting slimmer by the second. Nobody up to any good had to rush up from behind on someone. As was all too often the case, Clint's suspicions were confirmed almost instantly.

The man who rushed Clint had a face that was as angry as it was ugly. A wide mouth full of crooked teeth yawned open like an animal's, and he let out a low snarl from the back of his throat. The sound came more from the exertion of keeping himself so low and trying to speed himself up so much now that he knew he'd been spotted.

Since his gun hand had been carrying the folded money, Clint reached out with his left hand just as the attacker had almost gotten to him. With that hand, Clint grabbed the man by the face and twisted his entire body around using his right foot as a pivoting point.

"Watch it," Clint said to Maggie as he turned around in her direction.

Maggie yelped a bit when she saw the attacker being redirected toward her, but that didn't keep her from doing as she was told. She hopped up and back while stretching both hands behind herself toward the wall she knew she'd find there.

Already, the attacker was trying to wrench himself out of Clint's grasp. Unfortunately for him, Clint had a hold on his head the way he might palm a melon and wasn't about to let go easily. With a desperate twisting motion, he managed to slip out of Clint's grip. He discovered only too late that he'd been let go just so he could slam into a nearby post.

Clint had already dropped the money and was looking around at the rest of the stable as the other man knocked front-first into the wooden beam. Even though he couldn't see any other immediate threats, Clint wasn't about to let down his guard just yet.

"Who are you?" Clint asked as the other man shook the stars from his eyes and wheeled around to face him. "What're you doing here?"

The attacker was in no mood to talk and instead snatched a long, wicked blade from a scabbard strapped to his hip. He had the knife out and was lunging forward with impressive speed, a vicious smile forming on his lips.

Although the attacker was fast, Clint was faster. He lifted both arms up so they were out of the blade's way as he quickly shifted his body sideways to present his attacker with a smaller target. The blade hissed by Clint's midsection, shredding a thin strip of his shirt along the way. Clint could feel the steel grazing his skin, but couldn't allow himself to think too much more about it.

When Clint shifted to face the other man once more, a warm trickle of blood made itself known along his stomach. There wasn't much pain, but what little he did feel at that moment, Clint used to move himself forward like fuel to a fire.

Reaching out with both hands, Clint stepped forward as if he meant to grab the attacker by the throat. That move was a feint, however, and the man with the knife took the bait perfectly.

Gripping the knife, the man leaned back and took a swipe with the blade that would have gutted Clint if he had intended on following through with the move he'd started. But Clint wasn't there to receive the knife, which left the attacker overextended as his arm swung through empty air.

Clint saw his opening when the attacker stumbled a bit at the end of his swing. Even before he thought of his next move, Clint's body was already going through the motions. It was instincts like that which separated good fighters from dead ones. Without even feeling his feet touching the floor, Clint found himself moving around behind the guy with the knife.

Clint had moved so quickly that the attacker was already taking a stab at the spot where his target had previously been. While the man might have seen Clint start to move, he wasn't quite fast enough to adjust to it and found himself swinging yet again into nothing. He wasn't about to make another mistake, however, and prevented himself from extending his arm as much as he had the last time.

But Clint was already in a prime spot and was able to move in without having to worry about feeling another sting from that blade. Again reaching out with both hands, Clint made a genuine attempt this time to grab hold of the man around the neck as well as by his knife arm. Clint's left arm made it around the other's throat, but was unable to catch hold of more than the sleeve of the arm he'd been after.

As soon as he felt himself getting choked, the attacker became desperate. His arm began swinging in unpredictable arcs before he'd managed to flip the blade around in his hand so that it was now gripped as if he meant to make a downward stab with it.

Rather than chop anything in front of him, the attacker

started jabbing the blade behind him. His first few attempts got nowhere near Clint, but he didn't have to see the man behind him to know that he was getting closer with every try.

Clint's eyes grew wide as the blade started whistling through the air toward him. What worried him more than anything was that he couldn't see which way the next attack was coming until it was already almost there. He couldn't exactly let the man go, either, since that would just put the whole thing back to square one.

The blade appeared like a flicker of light in the corner of Clint's eye. It came less than an inch from his leg and even brushed against his knee on its way back. Even as he cinched in his grip around the man's neck, Clint could tell that another stab was on its way.

He was right. The blade came into view in a tight arc aimed directly at Clint's ribs. It was too late to let the man go or even push him away. It was even too late to try and twist away from the incoming blade. All Clint could do now was tighten his grip around the attacker's neck and pray to God that it would be enough.

TWENTY-FIVE

For Clint, the moment came at him as if it had been slowed down so he could see every bit of it. He watched as the blade came swinging toward him, but was powerless to do anything about it since he was going just as slowly as everything else. His muscles tensed, and he damn near lifted the other man off the ground, but that knife still kept coming.

Suddenly, the moment was knocked back into regular time. Actually, the moment wasn't the only thing being knocked around since the man in Clint's grasp was lifted even higher. Clint could feel some sort of impact thumping through the other fellow and before he figured out what it was, he felt something brush against him as well.

It was something that brushed against the inside of one leg, but came at him with enough force to send a small jolt through that kneecap. That jolt was nothing, however, compared to the jolt felt by the man in front of him.

The air was filled with a grunt that was pulled up from the other man's boots. Clint could feel the guy contracting until the arm around his neck was the only thing holding the man up. Once the man crumpled forward a bit, Clint could see the source of this peculiar turn of events.

Maggie was directly in front of both of them. Her face was constricted into an intense visage and both of her hands were balled into fists. One leg was supporting her weight while the other had swung straight up into an arc that slammed her shin into the knife-wielder's groin. She stepped in to kick so deeply that part of her swing had grazed Clint. Once he saw how badly the other man had it, Clint hardly even minded the little bit of pain in his kneecap.

That kick took every last bit of wind from the man's sails. His swing still came, but it veered off course so much that only the back of his hand made contact with Clint's ribs. Before that even happened, his grip had become too weak to keep the blade from slipping out through his fingers.

Clint winced as he let go of the man's throat. There was no need to hold on to him any longer since fighting had suddenly become the last thing on the fellow's mind. "Jesus," Clint said as he kicked the knife into a nearby pile of hay. "That hurt me just thinking about it."

Maggie stood her ground, watching the other man with a grin on her face as he dropped to his knees and grabbed his crotch with both hands. She looked over to Clint with a vaguely concerned expression. "I thought you needed some help."

"Oh, I did. It's just that . . ." He trailed off, glancing down at the man as he tried to pull in a shaky breath and had to hack it out again a second later. "Never mind. It's hard to explain."

Shrugging, Maggie raced over to where Clint had kicked the knife and dug it out of the hay. She turned the blade over a few times in her hands before stalking toward the coughing, suffering man on the floor. "This is one of Paul's boys," she said with a snarl.

"Are you certain?"

She nodded. "Yep." Holding the blade out until the

sharpened steel touched the other man's neck, she asked, "Aren't you?"

"Y . . . yeah. I w . . . work for Paul."

Clint winced again, sharing the other man's pain even though that same man had been trying to kill him only moments ago. Thinking about that brought Clint back to business and he knelt down while gently easing the knife in Maggie's hand to one side.

"Take it easy there," Clint said to her. Turning to look at the man, Clint took hold of the guy's shirt and shoved him so that he was sitting propped up against a nearby post. "How many of you are here?"

"Just me," the man said weakly while shaking his head. "Just me."

"That don't mean anything," Maggie said. "He could be lying."

Clint chuckled under his breath and said, "I don't think so. He's in too much pain to lie right now."

"You think so?"

"Yeah. I know so. The only man who can take a kick like that and still have much fight in him is a eunuch." Just to drive his point home, Clint made a quick, flinching movement toward the man's lower body.

As expected, the guy curled up as though he were expecting a bullet to punch through his gut. Clint looked back up to Maggie and saw that he'd made a firm believer out of her.

"Why don't you get our friend here some water?" Clint said.

Grudgingly, Maggie walked farther into the stables and found a dented tin cup to dip into one of the horse troughs.

Clint remained down close to the man's level, but was sure to keep out of arm's reach. That much precaution was more instinct than anything that was truly necessary. After all, the guy was still having a hard time sucking in a breath without sputtering and coughing.

"All right," Clint said. "Let's talk."

TWENTY-SIX

The conversation was short, yet very fruitful. For the most part, it was Clint who did most of the talking as he asked question after question while the man on the ground tried to drink his water without hacking it up. Maggie stood to one side and watched with her arms folded across her chest and her eyes narrowed into angry slits.

When Clint stood up again, he got some rope that was hanging from a nail in the wall and wrapped up the other man like a Christmas package. He took his time and the other fellow was in no shape to fight back. He did start to fuss once, but all he needed to see was a warning glance from Maggie before he coughed and gave in.

"What did he say?" Maggie asked as Clint walked toward her.

Ignoring her question, Clint asked, "Can you get this man to the law or would you like me to stick around to help out?"

Maggie's head cocked back as though she couldn't quite believe what she'd heard. Before the anger took over her face completely, she stepped in front of Clint to bar his way and said, "I asked you a question, Clint. What did he say to you?"

"Didn't you hear?"

"Not all of it. There was something about a station."

"That was a good portion of it."

"Hey," Maggie said as she stepped to one side so she could block Clint before he walked around her. "What's the matter with you? I helped you out, so why are you treating me like this?"

Clint's features softened a bit as he reached out to place both hands upon her shoulders. "You did help me out, Maggie. I thank you deeply for it. If I'm short with you, it's just because there's things I need to do and time is a factor."

"Where are you going?"

"It's probably best that you don't know."

"I want to come with you."

Hearing that stopped Clint in his tracks. He'd been just about to walk out of the stables with Eclipse's reins in hand when he froze. Slowly, he looked over his shoulder and studied Maggie intently before he asked, "What was that?"

"I want to come with you," she replied. "Take me with you."

Clint's head was already shaking before the last of her words came out. "No, Maggie. You wouldn't . . . you just . . . no."

"I wouldn't what, Clint?" she asked angrily. "It's just that what?"

Clint had a few ideas of what he wanted to say, but knew better than to say them. Either they didn't quite fit what he was thinking, or they might have ended up with him on the floor right next to the man tied up and nursing an aching crotch.

"I managed to avoid letting things get too out of hand," Clint said. "But that doesn't mean that there won't be danger involved."

Maggie nodded. "Oh I see? You mean dangerous like a lunatic swinging a blade at you or trying to kick the shit out of you in a saloon? I'd say it was a bit late to avoid that kind of danger."

"Actually, I meant the kind of danger where bullets are flying and one wrong step could mean the end of your life," Clint said with a deadly serious tone. "That's what I mean."

Maggie stopped herself from talking when she took a quick look over to see that the man tied to the post was watching and listening intently. She then stepped close enough to Clint so that he could hear her when she spoke in a fierce whisper.

"I know it'll be dangerous, Clint, but I want to go with you anyway. I can help you. I could scout ahead or get people to talk to me. You know damn well that men will let more slip when they're around a woman. Wouldn't that be useful?"

Clint had been looking deeply into her eyes and found a fire there that had nothing at all to do with the recent scuffle. By the looks of it, that fire had been burning there for some time.

"Why is this so important to you, Maggie?" he asked, making sure to keep his voice down to a whisper as well.

She lowered her eyes for a moment, took a breath, and then looked up at him again. "I take it you know that Paul Castiglione is more than just some crooked businessman."

"Yeah, I kind of figured that much."

"Well, my older brother used to run a turquoise mine in New Mexico. It wasn't much, but it made enough of a profit to help out the entire family." She took a deep breath. "When the money stopped coming, me and the family here in Labyrinth thought that he was just running through a dry spell. We got the news a month or so later that my brother had been killed and his mine was stolen right out from under him."

"Was it Castiglione?" Clint asked.

"There was never official word, but we eventually heard

from someone who knew my brother that it was some two-bit gunman from around here who did it. Not too much later after that, Paul shows up with money in his pockets and a big ol' smile on his face. That bastard even bragged in a saloon about how he made so much money in mining."

"But do you know it was him for certain?"

"No, and it's been driving me insane ever since. If you're going after Paul, he might start trouble for you and it could turn bad for one of you. If he dies, I'll never know for certain. If you die . . . well . . . I just wouldn't want that to happen. Please let me come with you, Clint."

When she saw that Clint was actually starting to consider the notion of her coming along, Maggie reached out and brushed the back of her hand along his cheek. "If you say no, you know I'll just follow you anyway. Then you'll have to worry about something happening to me when I'm out of your sight."

"That's not fair," Clint muttered. "And I don't exactly worry about every living thing that I can't see."

Maggie's smirk faded a bit and a genuine look of despair started to cloud her features.

"All right," Clint said. "But you have to do what I say when I say it."

"Of course," she said, brightening up instantly.

"Good. First, start by getting the sheriff to cart this fella out of here."

TWENTY-SEVEN

Cali Station was only a few days' ride from Labyrinth. Although he'd been reluctant to bring Maggie along at first, Clint soon found that he was glad to have her with him. First of all, she was excellent company and made the nights in camp some of the best in recent memory. Secondly, and more practically, she had plenty to say about Paul Castiglione.

Apparently, she'd tried to do some digging on the man when she'd first heard about her brother. The only problem was that she hadn't found much. Still, she'd gained some valuable insight along the way that could prove valuable.

"Paul's a gambler," she said toward the end of their ride. "Not just a regular gambler, but the kind that gets himself into trouble. He tried to make a name for himself as a card player, but nearly lost his shirt in the process.

"He's also a killer. I don't know what you might have heard about him and I don't care what can or can't be proved to the law," she said. "Him and those others he runs with are killers and they won't hesitate to kill again. My guess is that the only reason you haven't seen more of that for yourself is because he knows who you are and what your reputation is."

Clint laughed under his breath. "Trust me, that reputation of mine won't do much when push comes to shove. In fact, it might just be some kerosene thrown onto a fire."

"Just watch your back. That asshole who snuck into the stables would have gotten around to some awful things if you hadn't shown up and he's not even the worst of the lot."

"Can you tell me anything about the men he's got working for him?"

Maggie's face pinched a bit in concentration until she finally had to shake her head. "I wish I could, but there's not much else I know. I tried asking the law about them, but was just told it wasn't worth my effort and sent along my way."

"Whoever said that was right. Some men don't take kindly to being checked up on like that."

"I don't care what they like. My brother was one of my best friends in this world. After losing him, I'd go through hell and back to put right what happened to him."

Clint looked over at her and wondered if he'd made a bad call in allowing her to come along for the ride. Vengeance was a messy thing. All too often, it was like a pit of quicksand that dragged down not only the person standing in the middle of it, but anyone else standing nearby as well. Still, although he could see some anger boiling inside of Maggie's eyes, he didn't see the sort of uncontrolled rage that fueled vengeance.

"If Paul was responsible for what happened to your brother, I'm sure it will come out along with the rest of his dirty laundry. If he wasn't, then we should be able to at least find out something. Either way, we'll try to put this to rest for you."

"You don't know how much I appreciate that, Clint. Even finding out the least little thing would help me sleep at night." She smiled, which was enough to put out a little bit of the fire within her. "You're a good man."

"Don't get all sentimental," Clint said. "We haven't

found out anything just yet. Besides, you may want to take that back if things go wrong and you start to regret me allowing you to be there for it."

"I know what I'm doing," Maggie said resolutely. "And I know the risks. I've watched Paul Castiglione strut around Labyrinth long enough to know what he's capable of."

"True, but watching and taking part are two different things. Just remember—"

She cut him off with a quick salute as she recited, "I do what you say when you say it, sir."

Clint rolled his eyes and grumbled under his breath. Even as he looked away from her to watch the trail in front of him, he could make out the teasing grin on Maggie's face. He had also noticed something else. Namely, his eyes were drawn to the pistol stuck under her belt and mostly covered by her shirt.

Clint had caught sight of the gun the previous night. Considering how close they'd been when they camped, he was amazed that she'd been able to keep the gun hidden for that long. Being proficient with the iron himself, Clint could tell by the way she had it tucked away that she was more concerned with hiding it than being able to get to it at a moment's notice.

After listening to how she talked about Castiglione, it wasn't much of a surprise that she would want to be armed. Oddly enough, Clint felt better knowing about the gun. For the time being, however, he figured Maggie could keep on thinking that she'd snuck the gun past him. Besides, they were getting too close to town to start another possible argument just yet.

TWENTY-EIGHT

Cali Station was an odd name for a town. Like plenty of other towns all across the country, its name only seemed odd until a man got there and saw the place for himself. When Clint and Maggie rode into town, the first thing they saw were the crumbling remains of a platform and building next to a set of railroad tracks.

There was a sign running across the top of the building, which was just as run-down as the structure itself. Upon close inspection, the sign labeled the building as a train station that had been in use some twelve years before. It didn't take such close inspection from there to see that the line running through that station ended in California.

What had happened to the station and why it had fallen into such disrepair was a matter best left to historians or locals who gave a damn. Once Clint saw that half of the sign had fallen away, leaving only "Cali" left from California, that was enough for him. Train stations didn't need much of a reason to be abandoned. Clint's business was elsewhere.

While Clint was no expert in lumber, his eye was sharp enough to see that the rest of the town was a whole lot newer than the station from which it had gotten its name. It wasn't quite as big as Labyrinth, but there were certainly just as many people walking along the streets. Before too long, Clint even started to think there were more.

It was late afternoon and the boardwalks were filled with people of all shapes, sizes, colors, and dress. They wove around each other as well as the wagons and horses that passed each other on the streets. The air was alive with voices and the clunking of wooden wheels against a pitted road. When Clint looked over to check on Maggie, he found her glancing around with a vaguely confused expression on her face.

"Where are all these people going?" she asked.

At first, Clint thought the question was strange. Then, after looking around a bit more, he found it strange that he hadn't thought of it himself.

While there were plenty of storefronts on either side of the street, most of them were either boarded up or simple businesses that wouldn't exactly garner the sort of attention that was coming from all these people. There were a few tailors and some land contractors. There was a printer, a newspaper office, and a small saloon on the corner. Those might have accounted for a quarter of the foot traffic.

Clint stood up in his stirrups so he could see farther down the street. From what he could tell, there were a few more businesses and stores here and there, but still no major attraction. As they rode down the street, Clint would occasionally stand up again so he could take a look down another path or look around a corner. When he finally sat back down for the last time, he was shaking his head.

"I don't . . ." he started to say.

Maggie waited for a moment and then looked over at him. "You don't what?" she asked.

Clint snapped his fingers and started digging in his pocket. Maggie tried to get his attention, but he was completely focused on the task at hand. Finally, he found the folded notes he'd taken at Meyer's office and flipped through them. When he got to a particular page, he sifted through the scribbled lines until he found the right one.

"Here it is," Clint said victoriously.

Maggie waited some more for an explanation, but all she got was Clint's beaming smile. At that time, it wasn't enough to placate her. "What?" she asked again, beginning to get angry. "What are you looking at?"

"Actually," Clint said while taking a look around to find some street signs and glance down a few more paths, "it might be easier if I just showed you."

Fortunately, he didn't have to wait long before he found the street he'd been looking for. Clint turned Eclipse in that direction and Maggie followed right behind him. They rode for another block or two as the foot traffic grew thicker around them. Just as he could see that Maggie was about to lose what little remained of her patience, Clint pulled Eclipse to a halt and pointed toward the end of the next street.

"There," he said. "That's what's been getting all the attention."

Maggie glared at Clint for another second before turning to get a look at what he'd been pointing at. What she saw was another street with a few more storefronts lining either side. A few of the businesses seemed to be more popular among the locals, but there still wasn't anything to warrant the grin on Clint's face.

"I don't see it," she said.

"Look at the end of the street."

She did and all she found was a wide open space with a few smaller buildings scattered around it. Actually, there were two rather large buildings. One of those appeared to be a stable and the other was a single level, flat building that was as big as a quarter of one of the smaller blocks they'd ridden past. There were doors lining the entire perimeter as well as several windows glinting in the afternoon sun.

More than that, it only took watching the place for a few moments to realize that the large, squat building was the source of most of the town's foot traffic. People walked in and out of that building like water flowing through a major river fork. The current went both ways, however, and spilled out into the rest of Cali Station.

"What is that place?" Maggie asked.

Clint held out the paper he'd been looking at and said, "Take a look for yourself."

Maggie looked at the paper and nodded. Now, she was wearing a smile similar to Clint's. "You think Paul's in there?"

"Not only that, but I think Paul's sinking most of the money he's been getting into it."

"How do you know that?"

"Because, as far as I can tell, it's the only business on this list that he's not actually taking money from."

Maggie looked up from the paper, toward the large space and distant buildings, and then back down to the paper. The words next to Clint's finger read, "Cali Downs Racetrack."

TWENTY-NINE

Cali Downs Racetrack had been in place for some time. In fact, the building itself looked to be only slightly newer than the station Clint had passed when he and Maggie had ridden into town. The planks forming each wall were splintered and warped from the heat and the glass in the windows were fogged after withstanding countless storms and hours of blistering heat.

The heat wasn't too bad on this day, however, which accounted for the crowds coming and going through the busy betting windows. The closer Clint got to the racetrack, the more he felt his own blood starting to pump a little faster.

Beneath his feet, the ground trembled with the impact of dozens of hooves. Faces all around him showed the thrill of victory, the agony of defeat, and practically every other emotion in between.

"Hell of a place," Clint said as he looked around to see how Maggie was doing.

She rode beside him with a somewhat grim look on her face. Although she seemed to be affected by the excitement as well, she was doing her best to fight it rather than let herself get too caught up. In response to Clint's question, she shrugged and said, "I guess so."

They arrived at the building where most of the activity was centered. Clint and Maggie both swung down from their saddles and tied their horses up to the closest post. From there, they wandered through the clubhouse and took stock of the flourishing business.

While it wasn't the biggest or finest racetrack Clint had ever seen, Cali Downs wasn't too bad considering it was practically stuck out in the middle of nowhere. It was doing a good business with plenty of bettors dropping off their money at the windows and fewer of them picking up any sort of winnings.

There. were a few sets of grandstands surrounding the track. As Clint looked out toward the open area where the actual races were held, he saw a wave of horses come charging into sight. When they passed by in a flurry of pounding hooves and frantic jockeys, waves of cheers erupted from the stands.

A smile had come back onto Clint's face. With that much speed, excitement, and emotion all balled up into such a short period of time, the reaction was out of his control.

"You look pretty happy," Maggie said with a bit of disgust under her breath. "You want to buy a drink and place a bet?"

"Don't worry about me," Clint said patiently. "I haven't forgotten why we're here. I just like the races."

"Do you realize where all these people's money is going?"

"Yes I do. And since today seems like a big day at the races, I doubt that Paul would want to miss it."

"You think he's here?" she asked.

Clint looked back over to her. "Why do you think I'm smiling?" He waited and watched as Maggie looked around to put together the same pieces. When she got back to him, she seemed a little embarrassed.

"I'm not a big believer in luck," Clint said as he started walking toward the row of betting windows. Maggie fell into step beside him and they both did their best to avoid getting bumped around too much as they approached the shortest line.

"Really?" Maggie asked. "Then why place a bet?"

"Because it's part of the fun. Also, it's been a long ride and I'm too tired to go looking all over this place for Paul or one of his boys. I figure if we stay out in the open for long enough, one of them will spot us."

"And if they don't?"

"Then we'll have a bit of time off our feet while we watch a race. Have you ever seen one?"

Maggie let out a quick laugh. "Have I seen a race? I work with horses for a living, Clint. Of course I've seen a race. Maybe not at a track like this one, but I used to run against my brother when we were kids down at a dried-up riverbed back home."

"Did you win?"

Maggie shrugged. "Maybe once or twice. Who remembers?"

"If you won, you would've remembered."

For a moment, Maggie recoiled as though she'd been stricken. Her mouth dropped open a bit and her eyes went wide. Despite all this, she smiled at Clint while shaking her head. That smile grew a little wider when she reached out to smack him good-naturedly on the shoulder. "I can't believe you'd say that!"

"Am I right or wrong?"

She still shook her head, but rolled her eyes eventually. "I busted my leg in two places."

"How many times?"

Sheepishly, she said, "Three times."

Clint didn't say another word. He was stepping up to the front of the line, grinning back at her in a way that said more than enough. When he saw the young man behind the counter look up at him, Clint placed his wager and took the ticket that was handed to him.

"I'm just kidding around with you," he said to Maggie. "Anyone who's ridden horses faster than something that pulls a plow has broken at least a bone or two." Waiting until he saw the grateful smile on her face, Clint added, "I don't know about three times, but—"

He was cut off by another quick backhand to his shoulder before stepping away from the window and walking toward the seats. Seconds later, he felt Maggie's arm slip around his own as she walked beside him and lifted her face toward the clear, blue sky.

"It is a beautiful day to watch a race," she said. "Part of me is hoping that we actually get to see one before Paul knows we're here."

"I hope that wasn't too big of a part," Clint said. When Maggie looked at him, he nodded toward a pair of men who'd separated themselves from the crowd so they could walk straight toward them.

One of them wasn't familiar, but the other stuck out like a sore thumb. In fact, Clint doubted there were many places that a man like Bull could hide.

THIRTY

Bull walked up to them as though he were a cat stalking two cornered mice. His smile was a cruel shift of his lips, and his strut became more pronounced as he slowed down to stand in the middle of Clint and Maggie's path.

"Looks like you picked the wrong town to stop for the night," Bull said in a smug tone.

Clint looked around as if he were surveying his surroundings for the first time. "Funny," he said, "but it looks like the right place to me."

"We'll just see about that. Mr. Castiglione would like to have a word with you."

Clint shrugged and motioned for Bull to lead the way. When the bigger of the two men had turned around, Clint took a closer look at Bull's companion. The other man was slightly shorter than Clint and was a thick mass of muscle. His hair grew in uneven clumps and his hand brushed against the side of his holster as if he'd forgotten it was there.

Judging by the look on his face, however, he knew plenty well that Clint's gun wasn't too far from his reach.

"Where is Paul?" Clint asked.

"Not far from here."

"Does he have another office around here?"

That question went unanswered. Either Bull hadn't heard it or he simply didn't want to say anything more. Another race was starting up and people were quickly moving to their seats or trying to get a good spot along the rail surrounding the track. As he walked past the track, Clint found himself glancing over that way as well.

"Still worried about your bet?" Maggie asked.

"Not really."

Before too long, the two gunmen led Clint and Maggie away from the crowd. They weren't far from the track, though. In fact, they were at a spot that was still close enough to feel the excitement of the races. Once Clint saw where they were, he could feel that excitement even more.

Maggie looked around, feeling more at home than she had for a while. The smell of straw was as familiar as her mother's cooking. The sight of horses milling about in their stalls almost made her forget that she was still walking behind a couple of fellows who earned their living using their fists as well as the firearms hanging at their sides.

Bull walked around the farthest corner of the stables, allowing his partner to remain behind to make sure that Clint and Maggie did the same. When Clint rounded that same corner, he had to stop short before walking straight into the familiar figure that was waiting for them there.

"Howdy," Paul said while leaning against the back wall of the stables.

Not too far behind Paul was a wide rectangular doorway covered by a split door. The top half was open all the way while the bottom half swung back and forth idly upon rusted hinges. Clint had no trouble at all picking out the figures lurking in the shadows just inside the stables. While he couldn't tell which of Paul's hired guns they were, the pistols strapped around their waists were easy enough to see.

The man who'd been with Bull stepped a few paces away from Paul while the big man himself circled around to stand behind Clint and Maggie. Bull blocked them in like a wall of meat with thick arms crossed over his chest.

"And here I thought I wouldn't be seeing your face for a while," Castiglione said. "Imagine my surprise."

"You're the one that bolted from Labyrinth, Paul," Clint said. "And I do imagine that you are pretty surprised. You seem like a man who's used to getting his own way."

"And what makes this any different?"

"Because I'm here," Clint pointed out. "Right where you didn't want me to be."

"Oh, I think I can handle your visit just fine."

"We'll see."

"So what the hell are you doing here, anyway?" Castiglione asked.

"Just taking in the race."

"You certain that's all?"

Clint shrugged before answering the question. He could feel that such evasive responses were getting under Castiglione's skin. For that reason alone, he kept serving them up. "I was a little curious since you picked up and ran out of Labyrinth in such a hurry."

"I didn't run nowhere," Castiglione said before Clint could get out another syllable. "I got plenty of things to tend to and this happens to be one of them." Leaning back and extending his arms to encompass the entire track, he added, "Quite a big one, if I do say so myself."

"And successful, too," Clint added. "Sure looks that way, anyhow."

"You're damn right it's successful. Now, since we both agree I got a successful business to run, how about we cut through the bullshit? State your business here, Adams, before I have you tossed out on your ass."

"All right," Clint replied, stepping up so he could stand almost toe to toe with Castiglione. "I tracked you down here to make sure you're not squeezing out illegal money from this place like you were in Labyrinth. If this is a legitimate investment, then more power to you. But if you're stepping on one person's back to get your money, then I'll see that you answer for it."

Castiglione kept his arms outstretched. This time, however, he seemed to be making a big shrug of his shoulders rather than trying to gather his property closer to him. "Answer for it? I told you that all my claims are legal. If you got some kind of problem, then—"

"Yeah, I do have a problem," Clint interrupted. He'd taken another step closer to Paul and none of his men were fast enough to stop him. Now that Clint was in his new spot, none of the men in sight seemed too anxious to move him from it, either.

"My problem is when someone like you takes advantage of good people and then has the gall to wave some legal loophole around as their only defense," Clint said in a firm, intense voice. "I know about all your other holdings, and I know that this is probably the one you've been saving up for the entire time."

"Oh, you know all that, huh?" Castiglione asked with a smirk that was twitching too much to pass for casual.

Behind him, a shot fired into the air and the thunder of hooves rumbled through the air. When the racehorses rounded the bend closest to the stables, the ground shook beneath everyone's feet. Clint and Paul stood facing each other, glaring into the other's eyes until the thunder had receded.

"If you got such problems," Castiglione said, "then why not take them to the law? You want to stay around here, then place a bet and enjoy yourself. Otherwise, you can keep your foul tongue to yourself and get the hell off my property."

Clint backed off a few steps as the thundering hooves got farther and farther away. Finally, the horses slowed down amid a chorus of cheers and disheartened shouts. The race was over.

"I already did place a bet," Clint said as he lifted the handwritten ticket he'd purchased.

In the distance, a man's voice hollered out through a megaphone, "And Blue Beetle is the winner!"

Flipping the ticket over, Clint smiled directly into Paul's face. Blue Beetle was the name printed on the ticket. The amount of the bet was enough to put another angry twitch into Castiglione's forced grin.

"And I definitely am enjoying myself," Clint said. "Now I just need to collect my winnings. Excuse me." With that, Clint extended his arm and waited until Maggie took it before walking back toward the betting windows.

After they'd put some space between themselves and Castiglione, Maggie leaned over to Clint and whispered, "How on earth did you pick that horse?"

"Simple. Castiglione owns it."

THIRTY-ONE

The closer they got to the betting clerks, the more excited
Maggie became. Clint could feel her grip around his arm
tightening with every step. He started to lose feeling in his
hand as they waited in line. Every second or two, Maggie
would shoot a quick glance back toward the stables and the
spot where they'd spoken with Castiglione.

"Is he still there?" Clint asked, not bothering to take his
eyes from the back of the person's head in front of him.

"Yep," Maggie replied under her breath.

"What about his hired muscle?"

Maggie strained her neck trying to get a look around or
through the crowd that flowed by the windows. Finally, she
turned back to Clint while finding some strength to tighten
her hold on him even more. "Looks like one of them is still
with him. I can't see the others."

"Don't worry about it," Clint said.

"Really? You think we're safe?"

"I think if he wanted to start something, he would have
done it when we were closer and I put my back to him.
Now, he'll probably wait awhile before trying anything."

Although the grip on his arm loosened up a bit, Clint

knew it wasn't because any of Maggie's worries were lifting. "That makes me feel so much better," she said sarcastically.

Clint shook his head. "Hey, you're the one who wanted to come along with me. Did you think we'd just stroll in, smack the back of Paul's hand and stroll out again?"

She didn't have much of a reply to that, so Maggie stayed quiet. Every now and then, she would glance around at the crowd, looking for any familiar faces or anyone who looked back at them for too long. When she shifted to take yet another look, she felt a gentle touch on her elbow.

"Try to relax," Clint said. "Now you're making me nervous."

"Shouldn't we be nervous?"

"Alert? Yes. Nervous? No. At times like this, nervous is just as bad as being scared. It may be the most sensible thing in the world, considering the circumstances, but it's not going to help matters."

"What do you suggest?"

"Just focus on what we're doing and where we need to be," Clint said. "Keep your mind clear and you'll figure out what to do as it comes." Suddenly, he snapped his fingers. "Think of it like riding a wild horse. If you try to plan it out too much, you'll just be tangling yourself up inside. You need to know what you're dealing with and just be ready to handle what comes your way."

At first, Maggie was scowling at that advice. Then she thought about it for a moment or two and started to nod. A comfortable smile came onto her face and her shoulders began to slowly lower down from where they'd been bunched up around her ears.

"There," Clint said, sensing the change in her immediately. "That's better isn't it?"

"Yeah. It is."

They were at the head of the line in another minute or two and Clint stepped up to the teller who sat behind the counter. Taking out the ticket he'd removed earlier, Clint set it down and slid it toward the thin, bespectacled man.

Initially, the man took the ticket and glanced at it the way he had been looking at all the others. He took a second look at it and nearly dropped it with a quick flinch.

"Good Lordy," the man said. "That's an awful good bet, mister."

Clint nodded. "I had a hunch about that horse."

"Well, this is for an awful lot of money. I need to check this with my boss."

Feeling Maggie start to tense up again, Clint nodded and shifted on his feet so the man behind the counter couldn't see her. "No problem. I'll wait right here."

As soon as the man left, Clint felt a tugging on his elbow.

"He's going to bring Paul over here," she whispered.

"Don't worry until there's something to worry about," Clint assured her. "Now just sit tight and remember what I told you."

She closed her eyes and concentrated so hard that even Clint could almost make out what she was thinking. Before too long, she nodded and relaxed one more time. She wasn't quite as relaxed as she'd been earlier, but it would have to do for now.

Clint kept an eye on the skinny clerk the entire time. So far, the other man had walked to the back of the room and was knocking on a narrow door. When the door opened, the clerk spoke to a man that Clint couldn't see and held out the ticket to be inspected.

Peeking out from the other room, Zack squinted toward the counter. Clint waited until the smaller fellow's eyes were on him before smirking and giving Zack a wave. He didn't have to hear what the smaller man had to say to know that it wasn't at all complimentary. But Clint kept his smile on all the same and watched as the clerk came walking back to the counter.

Even before the skinny fellow made it back to his seat,

the apprehension was plain enough to spot in his face and the way he walked. Clint's ticket was still clutched in his hand, but it was trembling slightly despite the fact that there was no breeze coming through the windows.

"I . . . uh . . . I'm afraid there's a problem, sir," the clerk stammered.

"What problem could there be?" Clint asked innocently.

"I'm not exactly . . . it's just that . . . well I was told . . ."

Clint watched the skinny clerk squirm as if he didn't have the faintest notion about what could be going on. Finally, when it seemed that the poor clerk was going to seize up altogether, Clint raised his voice so that it was sure to be heard by anyone in the vicinity. "Are you saying you're not going to honor my bet? I placed it and won fair and square!"

"Please, it's not that, it's just—"

"Oh, I think that's it exactly!"

While the clerk was trying to come up with something to say next, a voice boomed from the area behind the row of windows.

"Give the man his money," Paul roared as he walked toward the narrow door where Zack was still glaring out at Clint. "What's the delay?"

The clerk turned to look over his shoulder, wincing as though there were a fist headed in his direction. "I was just told that—"

"Forget whatever anyone else said," Paul interrupted. "I own this place and we own up to our winners." He then nodded and looked around at all the people who were lined up and watching the exchange with no small amount of interest. "This is an honest place," Paul said in a bit more of a subdued tone. "Pay the man."

Clint put on a shocked expression and looked around to the audience that he'd been playing to the entire time. He sputtered as though he didn't know what to say and when he looked back to the clerk, he found Castiglione standing right behind the skinny fellow.

"It was a sizable bet, Mr. Adams," Paul said with a snake's grin. "I can pay you most of it now and have the rest delivered to you tonight."

"That sounds reasonable," Clint said.

"Where can I find you?"

"Well, we haven't exactly decided on a place to stay just yet."

"The Range Rider is nice," the clerk squeaked.

Clint nodded, savoring the angry twitch that came onto Castiglione's face. "Then that's where I'll stay. Have the rest of the money sent there. I'll expect it tonight."

"All right then," Castiglione said, playing the part of good host to the onlookers. "And congratulations." Lowering his voice so he wouldn't be heard now that most of the other people nearby were getting back to their own business, he added, "Now get the hell out of here."

For the moment, Clint was plenty happy to oblige.

THIRTY-TWO

"Oh my God, that was one of the most exciting things I've ever done in my whole life!"

Maggie had been about to burst the entire time since they'd left the racetrack and headed to the Range Rider Hotel. Every step of the way, she'd been looking over her shoulder, commenting on the way Paul looked when he handed over his own money to Clint. Every now and then, she took Clint's hand and squeezed it so hard that he almost heard the popping of his bones.

Now that they were inside the hotel, she couldn't contain herself for one more second. The statement came out like an explosion, drawing the attention of everyone standing in the large, clean lobby of the hotel. Clint looked around at the amused faces staring back at them and shrugged.

"We just had a big win at the track," he explained.

That seemed to be enough to satisfy the others in the lobby because they chuckled among themselves and got back to what they'd been doing before Clint and Maggie had arrived.

The hotel was set up like a ranch house. It was flat and wide with plenty of open space. There was a second floor, but it was only another level of rooms forming a ring around the center of the building. In that center was a large desk covered by a register, papers and pencils, as well as a few copies of the daily newspaper.

Behind the desk was a man who fit in perfectly with the decoration of the hotel itself. He was dressed up in rugged browns that seemed comfortable, well-worn, and a bit dusty. A welcoming smile appeared beneath his bushy mustache, which also seemed to go along just fine with the feel of the hotel.

"Won big, did ya?" the man behind the desk asked.

"It's bound to happen every now and then," Clint replied.

"Wish it could happen every so often for me. The only way I see any winnings from that track is when folks like you come through here."

"Well, I'm expecting a delivery from the track some-time tonight." Peeling off a bill from his winnings and slid-ing it across the desk, he asked, "Be sure to keep a lookout for me, will you?"

The man's hand reached out to cover the bill and pull it in. After glancing down to see how much he'd been given, the clerk grinned and nodded. "Will do. I assume you'll be staying here? We have the Honeymoon Suite available."

Clint glanced over to Maggie. Although it seemed that she couldn't have been more excited before, now she seemed positively ready to explode. Her eyes fixed on him expectantly and both hands were clenched up close to her mouth.

"Why not?" Clint said. "Seems like as good a time as any to celebrate."

"Why not, indeed?" the clerk said. He was wearing a smile almost as big as Maggie's as he stepped over to a wall covered in hooks with keys dangling from them. Judg-ing by the amount of dust on the wall and the key itself, it had been an awfully long time since anyone had felt like celebrating that much.

When he turned back around, the clerk saw that Maggie had practically leapt into Clint's arms and was smothering him with a kiss. He waited until Clint was free again before holding out the key. Moments before Clint got the key in hand, the clerk winced and pulled his hand back an inch or two.

"Actually," the clerk said hesitantly, "you might want to get a look at our rates before taking your things up to the Honeymoon Suite."

Clint studied the pained expression on the clerk's face before studying the sheet of paper he was shown. Normally, the rate for that suite would have made Clint's heart skip a beat. For that price, he should have been able to rent a floor of rooms for the night, complimented by a fine dinner and several dancing girls as well.

This time, though, Clint winked and pushed the paper back. "The suite will be just fine. Be sure to have some wine sent up and a hot bath drawn as well."

"Yes, sir!"

"When I get my delivery tonight, be sure to come and get me as soon as possible."

The clerk couldn't move fast enough now to make the arrangements and agree to everything that came out of Clint's mouth. "Of course, sir!"

"I'll just go fetch our bags."

When Clint turned around, there was a veritable army of boys ranging from the ages of ten to thirteen years of age.

"Just tell us where they are, mister," the oldest boy said. "We'll get your bags right quick."

Clint smiled and nodded. It was good to live the high life every now and then. Especially when it wasn't his money that was flying out in every direction.

THIRTY-THREE

By the time Clint and Maggie had taken their time walking to their room, the army of youthful helpers was already storming up the stairs with their saddlebags in tow. Actually, since there weren't many bags to carry, the army had been whittled down to its senior members. The two oldest boys rushed at Clint and came to a skidding stop to drop the saddlebags onto the floor.

"Here you . . . go, mister," the thirteen-year-old said between heaving breaths. "Anything . . . else we can . . . do for you?"

"Go get something to drink and catch your breath," Clint said. Handing out some more of the money he'd won from Castiglione, he added, "And get something for the rest of that group of yours while you're at it."

Both of the kids' eyes widened to the size of saucers as they clutched the money in their hands. When they looked up to Clint, they found him glaring down at them sternly.

"And don't let me hear about you keeping all that for yourselves," Clint warned. "Share it among all those that were with you before."

"Yes sir," the thirteen-year-old said earnestly. "We will. Honest."

Unable to hold his stern expression any longer, Clint patted the kids on their heads and sent them on their way. "What?" he asked when he saw the way Maggie was looking at him.

"That was sweet," she said.

Clint shrugged and fitted his key into the door. "Making that call on Paul's horse was about one step above cheating the way I see it. The only thing that straightens things out is if I give the money back to the town he stole it from in the first place."

"Like Robin Hood?" Maggie asked, her smile getting warmer and her head tilting at a loving angle.

"Actually, I was thinking more of pissing off Castiglione," Clint said as he turned the key in the lock and opened the door. "But whatever works for you is fine by me."

The door swung open to reveal so much open space that Clint thought he was about to step outside again. The suite was easily the size of half a dozen normal rooms. Nearly every inch of the floor was covered by a burgundy carpet and the windows were covered with fancy velvet curtains. Every table in sight was carved from mahogany and even the wash basins were accented with strips of gold.

Even the air from inside the room smelled expensive, scented with the food that had been eaten there and imported candles that had long ago burned out.

Clint and Maggie were still standing at the door, gaping in wonder at where they were going to spend the night. When both of them were done taking their first, lingering look, their eyes wandered back toward each other.

"Are you going to carry me over the threshold?" Maggie asked.

"For what I paid for this room, someone should carry us both."

Before Clint could say another word, he saw Maggie make a quick move toward him. After taking half a step, she wrapped her arms around the back of his neck and jumped up with both feet. His arms came out reflexively to catch her and a few stumbling steps brought them both into the Range Rider's most expensive suite.

Maggie kicked the door shut before leaping out of his arms so she could run around the room and check out every last corner. Clint had to reach outside to bring their bags inside and once he set them down, he had to take one more look around.

The place was so big, it was ridiculous. In fact, the suite was made up of two rooms, divided by a padded screen painted in a way to make it look as if it had come from the Far East. Clint was no expert, but he knew enough to be certain that Kentucky was about as far east as that divider had ever been. That notwithstanding, he still found himself marveling at the luxury that was his for the next night or two.

He wasn't the only one admiring the accommodations. The last he'd seen of Maggie, she was practically dancing in the room and lending an occasional twirl to her steps. The curtains ruffled every now and then as she pulled them to one side so she could take a look at the street below.

While she was admiring the view, Clint was glancing outside as well for different reasons. He wanted to see which streets the suite overlooked, which buildings looked into their room, and if he could spot anyone spying on them at the moment.

The streets outside of their room were busy, but the crowds were thinning out since the last of the races were finishing up. It looked as though a few stores and maybe even a poker hall was close to the Range Rider and as far as Clint could tell, there wasn't anyone watching the room just yet.

"When do you think the rest of your money will be here?" Maggie asked from another part of the room.

Clint was sifting through his saddlebags and taking out some clothes that needed to be washed. Since he meant to blow all of what he'd won, he might as well catch up on some laundry. "I doubt Paul will want to be too prompt about it. Probably sometime after supper."

"Do you think it was a good idea to tell him where you were staying?"

"If I didn't tell him, he would have just found out on his own anyway. That reminds me. We shouldn't expect a friendly delivery. I'm pretty sure that Paul will be sending over his boys with something else for me besides a stack of money."

"But you don't think that will be for a while?"

Clint thought it over for a moment before shaking his head. Since Maggie still wasn't in his sight, he said, "No. He's going to want to let me stew for at least a few hours. He's a deliberate man, so he'll want to scout out a few things before he makes any sort of move."

"Good," Maggie said as she stepped out from behind a screen. "Because there's a few moves I want to make, and I can't wait another second."

Clint drank in the sight of her as she stepped into view. Her straight blonde hair fell over her shoulders and her eyes were fixed intently upon him. The only thing she wore was a thin, form-fitting undershirt and the hungry smile upon her face.

THIRTY-FOUR

Clint was so taken aback by the sight of Maggie's body that it took him a few seconds to realize that she'd been closing all the curtains as she'd made her rounds through the suite. Reaching behind him without taking his eyes off of her, Clint tugged on a few drawstrings to close the two sets of curtains closest to him.

Maggie stalked toward him like a cat. Every muscle in her body shifted beneath her skin as she moved. The bit of light trickling into the room caressed her every curve. The thin undershirt she'd left on was so tight that it looked more like a layer of cream that had stuck to her upper body. Pert nipples poked at the fabric as she approached him, and had become fully erect by the time she made it to the spot where Clint was standing.

Clint reached out with both hands to hold her by the waist as she stepped up to him. His eyes worked their way slowly down her body, lingering at the flat muscles of her stomach before sliding lower to the soft patch of hair between her legs.

The curve of her waist was gentle and smooth. He could feel her breaths quickening as he allowed his hands to trace a line up and down her sides. As she stepped in closer to him, Maggie tightened her hold on Clint until she was pressed up tightly against his chest.

With her in such an embrace, Clint slipped his arms around her and looked down along the line of her back. Maggie's firm buttocks came out at a slight curve as well and felt supple and round when he placed his hands upon them. She let out a little sigh as she squirmed against his chest, settling into a perfect spot.

Clint slid his hands up along her back until his fingers slipped underneath the bottom of her undershirt. The thin cotton peeled away from her body as Clint walked her toward the bed while easing the one remaining garment from Maggie's frame.

By the time the backs of her legs bumped against the edge of the bed, all she had to do was lift her arms and slide out of the shirt while lowering herself down onto the mattress. A warm, hungry smile was still on her face as she continued to lower herself onto the bed, extending her arms up over her head as she came to a rest.

Clint shook his head while admiring her naked body. Maggie's bare breasts heaved with every breath. Her feet slid up to brace against the baseboard and she opened her legs slightly as she scooted back onto the mattress.

Clint had already started unbuttoning his shirt, but forced himself to move even faster when he got a look at the way Maggie waited for him. She kept her eyes closed while slowly wriggling on the bed, savoring the feel of the blankets against her naked skin.

In no time at all, Clint was naked as well and climbing on top of her. When she opened her eyes, Maggie found him looking straight down at her, wearing nothing but a hungry smile of his own.

"Well hello there," she whispered. "It feels like I've been waiting for this for a long time." Reaching between his legs, she immediately found his erect penis and let her fingers slide up and down its length while pulling in a slow breath. "Feels like you're just as happy as I am to finally be here."

"Oh yeah," Clint whispered. "Happy just doesn't quite cut it."

Maggie's smile became a seductive grin as she closed her eyes, arched her back slightly, and opened her legs. "Just wait," she purred while guiding him between the smooth, wet lips of her pussy.

With a gentle push of his hips, Clint slid inside her. He let out the deep breath he'd been holding as he felt himself become enveloped by her moist embrace. As he drove all the way inside of her, Clint felt Maggie's legs wrap around him. Her ankles locked at the small of his back so she could pull him in even farther.

Once he'd buried every inch of his rigid penis inside of her, Clint stayed where he was so he could savor the moment. He opened his eyes to find Maggie still languishing in the sensations he was causing. Easing out of her and pumping back inside, Clint watched as her face changed in response to even the slightest movement of his body.

Just when it seemed that she was about to catch her breath, Clint took it away again when he picked up his pace and took on a rhythmic thrusting between her thighs. Maggie's legs closed tightly around him. Her eyes clenched shut and she started moaning softly every time his body pressed against hers.

Clint's hands wandered up and down the length of her body. Sometimes, he would linger at her hips so he could cup her tight backside while pumping into her. Sometimes, he would run the palms of his hands along her sides until he could cup her breasts and tease her nipples until she started to tremble with appreciation.

Finally, Clint's hands moved along the length of her arms until he was able to lace his fingers through Maggie's. From there, they held on tightly to each other as their hips writhed against each other in perfect unison.

Their limbs started to entangle around the other until both of them started to be taken over by pure instinct. Maggie's movements became almost desperate beneath Clint's body until she was able to roll him onto his side. He slid out of her for a second and her face immediately reflected her instant longing for his return.

After draping one leg over Clint's side, Maggie was able to line herself up to him again. She pulled in a quick breath when she felt him enter her again. That breath was soon caught in her throat again as her eyes widened in surprise. Clint had found another sensitive spot within her thanks to their new position and every muscle in Maggie's body tensed as his hard cock brushed back and forth against it.

She grabbed on to him with all of her strength, straining against him as her orgasm threatened to overtake her. When she was finally brought over the edge, Maggie pressed her face against Clint's chest and let out a shuddering moan that he could feel as well as hear.

Clint felt her tighten around him, bringing him closer and closer to his own climax. Once Maggie's orgasm had started to recede, she leaned back and had a look of such fatigue on her face that it made Clint grow even harder within her.

Despite the sweat that formed on her brow and the tiredness in her eyes, Maggie still writhed against him. Her moans grew again in intensity as he continued to pump between her legs. Every breath was straining and her eyes shot open as she was quickly brought to the edge of a second climax.

Clint grabbed hold of her and pushed all the way inside before rolling Maggie once again onto her back. She propped one leg up and draped the other across the small of his back, holding on to his shoulder with every bit of her fading strength.

Looking down at her as he pounded into her, Clint saw

her reacting to every last bit of sensation. She squirmed beneath him as though she were dreaming, yearning to be pushed over the edge one more time, yet unsure if she could handle so much pleasure at once.

The orgasm came, not just for her but for Clint as well. He could feel it stirring at the base of his spine before working its way through his entire body. After a few more powerful strokes, he exploded inside of her. Clint's hands tightened around Maggie's and he clenched his eyes shut tightly as the climax swept through him.

When it passed, he had to force himself to let go of her hand. Opening his eyes, he saw that Maggie was just as breathless as he was. Clint shifted to one side and dropped onto the mattress beside her. Neither of them tried to speak. Instead, Maggie curled up beside him with one hand tracing patterns across his bare chest.

Clint lay back and enjoyed the moment. It wasn't too often that one so perfect came along.

THIRTY-FIVE

The day rolled by and found its way into the night. The sun drifted down into the west and the air took on a slight chill. All in all, it wasn't anything out of the ordinary. It was just another race day in Cali Station. With the track emptied out, the town had taken on a quieter feel. There were fewer bodies crowding the boardwalks and fewer horses clogging the streets.

Clint took notice of the way the town emptied out, figuring that a good number of the people he'd seen earlier had been there strictly for the races. While some of them had probably left town altogether, he figured a good portion of them were still kicking about. More than likely, they could be found gambling away their winnings or trying to recoup their losses at one of the local saloons.

Even likelier was the fact that those gamblers were still handing over their money to Paul Castiglione one way or another.

Clint stood in his room next to an open window. He'd gotten himself dressed, but hadn't scraped up the gumption to leave the suite. Instead, he studied the town from his window and watched as night fell around him. Not too far away, Maggie bathed in a tub that had been brought up into

141

the room. Despite their recent lovemaking, she insisted on
bathing behind the screen.

"You sure you don't want to join me?" she called out.

Clint smirked. "I'm sure." He was going to mention
how it was getting well past the time that they could both
relax, but held his tongue. Surely she hadn't forgotten
about why they were there. Mentioning it then would have
just put her on edge.

Best to let Maggie relax while she still had the chance.
Odds were real good that neither of them would get another chance once things truly started rolling.

As if reacting to that chain of thought, a knock sounded
from the door. Clint glanced in that direction and slowly
turned to face it. He'd strapped the modified Colt around
his waist awhile ago, but still let one hand drop to brush
against the familiar iron.

The knock came again. This time, it was a little quicker
and a little harder against the door.

"Mr. Adams," came the familiar voice of the front desk
clerk. "Mr. Adams, are you still . . . um . . . available?"

Clint reflexively put his back to the wall rather than the
window and walked toward the door on the balls of his feet.
Even though so much open space in one room tended to
make any sound that much louder, Clint managed to get to
the door without more than a slight rustle of feet against
the floor.

When he arrived at the door, he reached down to take
hold of the handle, but refrained from doing anything else.
Rather than open the door, he leaned against it so he could
better hear what was happening on the other side.

All he could hear was the impatient shuffling of feet and
someone clearing their throat. Although the clerk sounded
a bit nervous, he didn't seem to be overly anxious. More
important, it seemed as if he was definitely alone.

Finally, Clint opened the door. As he'd figured, the clerk
was standing in the hallway all by himself. His cheeks

were flushed and he reflexively tried to avert his eyes from anything but Clint himself.

"Glad to catch you at a . . . well . . . better time," the clerk stammered.

"Why wouldn't it be a good time?" Clint asked.

"Well, when your bathtub was brought up, I heard that your companion was a little . . . shall we say . . . disheveled."

The clerk shifted from nervous to suggestive in the blink of an eye. He nudged Clint slightly and gave him a look that was normally shared between two boys at their first time in a cathouse. Clint recalled Maggie answering the door while pulling on her clothes, but apparently she'd given the staff a little better show than he'd thought.

"Right," Clint replied without returning the clerk's lecherous grin. "What can I do for you?"

Clearing his throat and returning to his normal businesslike manner, the clerk said, "You mentioned that a package should be arriving for you?"

"I did."

"Well, it's here."

Clint held out his hand. "Fine. I'll take it."

"Actually, it needs to be delivered to you personally. Mr. Castiglione is downstairs. He insisted on it."

The clerk nodded toward the top of the stairs and Clint leaned out to look in that direction as well. He had barely taken half a step through the door, but that was enough for his head to clear the room. He spotted some quick motion from the corner of his eye, but it was too late to do much about it.

The next thing he felt was a dull, smashing impact against the back of his head. As he started to topple forward, Clint's entire world faded to black.

THIRTY-SIX

Clint's head was pounding when his senses started to come back to him. His ears felt like railroad spikes that had not only been driven through his skull, but were also ringing from the impact of the hammer. Sounds rushed to him in a wave and he knew he was still a few seconds away from making any sense of them.

His vision was coming back, but only in the form of some light piercing through the fog that had swept in to envelop him. As for everything else, he felt as if he were sliding down a rocky slope with his back scraping against rugged terrain.

He pulled in a breath, which did him some good. With his reflexes screaming at him to wake up, Clint tried to move but found that he couldn't even budge his arms.

There was a clunking sound that rattled his brains as well as a wheezing rush that reminded him of air passing through a funnel. He could move his legs, but that only seemed to be because they were dangling already. While that was somewhat promising, it only worsened the sensation of falling.

Suddenly, that sensation started to ease up. He was no longer falling and the rush in his ears was tapering off as well. He still couldn't move his arms, but that wasn't from lack of trying. Enough of his senses were flooding back to him for him to know that something was keeping his arms from moving.

A second later, he realized that his initial reactions hadn't been too far off.

While he wasn't falling, Clint figured out why he felt that scraping against his back and the dangling sensation in his legs. He was being dragged. And whoever was doing the dragging was doing so by pulling Clint by the arms.

Energized by a quick breath, Clint blinked his eyes a few times and was able to clear away some of the cobwebs. His head was still aching like a son of a bitch, but that pain was at least something solid for him to grab on to and ride all the way back to consciousness.

The first thing Clint saw once his vision cleared was the hallway where he'd been knocked out. He saw that through another doorway, but at least that meant he hadn't been out for more than a few seconds. He couldn't see or hear anyone else, but Clint still thought that made it a toss-up as to whether or not there were others in the room besides the one who'd bushwhacked him.

Even if there were a dozen men in that room, however, that didn't change the fact that Clint had to move quickly while there was still a chance of tipping the odds back into his favor. He kept his body loose and gave himself another couple of seconds to wait for an opening. If one didn't come in that time, he would just have to make an opening for himself.

Luck was on Clint's side. Not long after he was brought to a spot inside the room, Clint's arms were dropped and he felt footsteps moving around the side of his head. Clint gave himself a two-count. After that, he saw a boot drop into his line of sight and he snapped his hand out to grab hold of it.

He must have been a better actor than he'd thought, because Clint took the other man completely off his guard. In fact, when Clint's hand closed around that man's ankle, he heard a surprised grunt come from what seemed like a mile or so over his head.

The ankle twisted out of Clint's grasp, but was still moving forward. Although he wasn't able to keep hold of it, Clint did manage to reach out a second time and push on that same heel at just the right time. The rest of the other man came into view as he stumbled forward while trying to keep himself from falling.

Clint took that opportunity to gather himself up and try to get his feet beneath him. Just as he got himself propped up, he saw something come at him from behind and to one side. It was another boot and it wasn't coming from the man who was about to fall awkwardly onto the floor.

Another difference this time was that Clint wasn't about to let himself take another kick to the head. Both hands came up from where they'd been holding him up to form an X in front of his head. The kick pounded against his crossed arms. Even more of the impact was absorbed by the fact that Clint's whole upper body was already starting to fall back toward the floor.

Pushing off with both arms, Clint shook off the kick and bounced up again as soon as his shoulder blades tapped against the floor. His energy was rushing back into him, aided by the fact that his heart was practically slamming his blood through his veins. In no time at all, Clint was rolling forward and springing onto his feet.

The room teetered about him for a second, but Clint was still able to get his bearings. A quick look around told him that he'd been dragged into a smaller hotel room and two other men were in there with him. The man he'd tripped up not too long ago was swinging around toward him while making a reach for the gun at his side.

Clint lunged forward, leading with his fist, which slammed powerfully against the other man's face. Pain shot through Clint's hand after cracking against the man's cheekbone, but it seemed that the other fellow was doing a whole lot worse.

As the first man reeled back, Clint pivoted around to get a look at the second. That one had stumbled back a step or two after his kick was deflected, but hadn't been thrown off too badly. Worse than that, he'd already had his gun drawn when Clint was being dragged into the room. An angry fire burned in his eyes, which flared up even more when he saw that Clint still hadn't been taken down.

Clint's eyes locked on to the gun in that second man's hand. He noticed the first moment that it started to come up toward him and he could feel the finger tightening around the trigger as though it were his own. Acting out of pure reflex, Clint's hand dropped down toward his holster. Only after starting the draw did he wonder if his gun would even be there.

The next few seconds moved like snails through molasses. In that time, Clint's mind bounced back and forth between the two distinct possibilities. Either his modified Colt would be there for him or it had been taken away as soon as he'd been knocked out.

The former meant he was still in the game, while the latter meant he was out.

Life or death.

It all came down to another toss of the dice.

Time surged forward at its normal speed the moment Clint's finger got its first feel of iron. The Colt was there and waiting for him. Apparently, the ambusher had figured on having a little more time before Clint woke up.

Clint cleared leather so quickly that he didn't even recall doing it. His arm worked on its own accord and soon the room was filled with the Colt's thunder. The man in front of him jerked back as though he'd been kicked by a mule. Blood sprayed through the air and he was gone.

Clint turned around to face the first man just as that one

was recovering from the punch he'd taken. Only now did Clint recognize the man's face. He was one of the bigger men who'd always been around Paul Castiglione, but it wasn't Bull. If Clint had a few moments, he might have remembered the guy's name. The man was definitely one of Paul's boys and that was all Clint needed to know.

The Colt left a wispy trail of smoke as it was brought around to point at the gunman. Clint's eyes fixed upon that one's face with such intensity that they almost seemed to smoke themselves.

"I was told you had something for me," Clint said in a tone that was just short of a growl. "Am I going to get the rest of my winnings or is Paul going to lose another lackey?"

THIRTY-SEVEN

The door to the suite came open and Maggie nearly jumped out of her skin. She'd been walking across the room wrapped in a towel with her hair pinned up in a bun. When she saw that it was Clint who'd walked in, she smiled and patted her chest.

"You frightened me," she said before turning back to her saddlebag. "How much of that money do you have left? If we're staying here much longer, I'd like to get some clothes."

Clint stood in the doorway with his heart still pounding. He felt as though he'd been dragged behind a runaway horse and doubted that he looked much better. His mouth gaped open a bit more when he realized that she truly was just going to fuss with her clothes awhile longer.

"Did you hear anything strange while I was out?" Clint asked.

Maggie was behind the screen, about to change into a fresh set of clothes. "I think someone might have tripped or dropped something, if that's what you mean."

"And did you notice that I was gone for a bit too long?"

"Actually, I think I fell asleep in the bathtub. That hot water felt so . . ." Maggie had peeked from behind the di-

149

vider and had finally taken a real look at Clint's face. "Oh my God!" she yelped. Dropping everything including the towel that had been covering her up, Maggie rushed over to where Clint was standing. "Are you all right?"

For a moment, Clint was relieved that she'd noticed the fact that he was bleeding and about to keel over. After that, he was just glad to have someone pull a chair close enough for him to fall into. "I've been better," Clint said. "But it could have been a lot worse."

"What happened?"

Clint filled her in on what had happened after he was lured out into the hall. Maggie listened while running back to get the towel she'd dropped. Instead of wrapping it around herself, she dipped one end into the bathwater and used it to clean the bloody wound on the back of Clint's head.

Wincing a bit as she touched the lukewarm water to his wound, Clint decided to glaze over the more exciting details of his scuffle. Maggie seemed to be worked up enough as it was.

Once he was done telling her the account, Clint asked, "How long was I gone?"

Maggie shook her head while dabbing away the last of the blood on his scalp. "I'm not certain. No more than a few minutes. I really did doze off for a bit. I'm so sorry."

"No problem. Actually, I'm glad you're all right and didn't have anyone . . ." Clint stopped himself as the rest of that sentence sank in before he even spoke it out loud.

What he meant to say was that he was glad nobody had come into the room after her. At that moment, Clint realized that if she'd been asleep, there very well could have been someone in there with them. When he got up, Maggie started to protest. Clint silenced her with a quick hand and got to his feet.

The Colt emerged from its holster with the whisper of iron against leather. Clint stalked around the room, checking every corner and anyplace big enough to conceal a man. He found nobody, however, so sat down into his chair one more time.

"There's nobody here," he said.

Maggie looked down and cringed as though she'd completely forgotten that she was naked. Hurrying over to her clothes, she threw them on and rushed back to where Clint was sitting. "What did those men want?"

"They didn't want to pay me my money, that's for sure."

"You said there was one left when it was over. Where is he? Tied up and waiting for a deputy to come collect him?"

"Actually, I got the clerk to keep this as quiet as he could for the time being. Since he was forced into luring me out into the hall in the first place, it didn't take too much convincing for him to do me a favor."

"And that favor was to get the law and clean up the body?"

Clint shrugged. "Not exactly."

"I don't like the sound of that." Maggie paused and when she saw that Clint wasn't about to say anything right away, she asked, "What did you do with him?"

"I let him go."

"What? After he just tried to kill you?"

"Tried is the important word here. He and his friend tried to kill me and now only he is limping back to Paul Castiglione. Making it through a fight by the skin of your teeth tends to rattle most folks, even the big talkers like Castiglione and his boys."

"That doesn't mean he won't be back," Maggie said. "And next time there will probably be a whole lot more of them."

"True. That is, if we waited around long enough for them to screw up enough courage to come back here."

Although she still looked nervous, Maggie didn't seem as shaky as she had a moment before. "What do you mean?" she asked.

"I let that one go, but it was only so he could deliver a message. I made it known that I want to have a word with Paul. Since this is coming after his boldest move against me, I'm thinking that he won't be so cocky. He might even be open to a suggestion or two."

Taking a deep breath, Maggie picked up the wet towel that she'd been using earlier and dabbed at another trickle of blood that was appearing on his neck. "I guess I shouldn't try to crowd you so much. You have more experience with this than I have."

Clint shrugged again. This time, he followed up by pulling Maggie closer until she had to sit on his lap. "I'd like to say that I know exactly what I'm doing, but you're too smart to buy into that. Let's just say I've got a plan."

"You do, huh? And does that have anything to do with this suggestion you were talking about?"

"It might."

"Well, I just wish I could be a part of it."

"Actually, I was just going to talk to you about that."

THIRTY-EIGHT

"Where's Sam?"

The stocky gunman shifted in front of Paul Castiglione like a nervous child. His face was a patchwork of different bruises and a few cuts. His lip was swollen and one eye was black as coal. Even so, it seemed as though having to answer Paul's question was more painful than anything that had left its mark upon his face.

"Sam's . . . Sam's dead," the gunman said.

Paul was silent for a moment. He then started glancing around at the few other men gathered in the room as though he wasn't sure he could trust his own ears. "Did you say he's dead? Speak up, Kyle. I don't think I could have heard you correctly."

Kyle nodded slowly at first, but then quicker when he realized that there was nothing else for him to do. "Yeah. You heard me just fine."

"What happened?"

"We went to the Range Rider just like you told us. We got the fella behind the front desk to draw Adams out. By the looks of it, him and that blonde were having a good ol' time."

Impatiently, Paul started waving his hand toward Kyle. "Yeah, yeah. Go on."

"Adams stepped out. I knocked him on the head and dragged him into another room, but he woke up before we could tie him up. He woke up before we could even get his gun from him."

Paul shook his head and pressed his fingertips against his closed eyes. "At least tell me you hurt the man."

"There was a fight and we tussled for a bit."

"Did you hurt him or not?"

Kyle paused before shrugging. "Probably not much."

"But he killed Sam?"

"Sure did."

"So tell me something," Paul said as he moved his hand and slowly opened his eyes. "If Sam's dead then that means he at least made a move against Adams. Tell me why you're still alive. Did you just turn tail and run the minute you saw him open his eyes?"

"Hell no," Kyle said vehemently. The fire in his eyes was short-lived and he was soon lowering them altogether. "He, uh, gave me a message to give to you."

"Let me guess. I need to leave town or he'll come after me?"

"No. First off, he asked for the rest of his money. When I didn't have it, he said he was gonna kill me. But he didn't kill me. Instead, he let me go just so long as I told you that he wanted to meet with you again."

"Meet with me?" Paul asked. He thought about it for a moment, but that only served to deepen the confusion upon his face. "Does he think I'll just walk into a meeting after he gunned down one of my men? Hell, I bet he even tried to get the law after me."

Hearing that last part caused most of the men in the room to start laughing. Paul's laugh was halfhearted at best. He seemed to be more interested in what Kyle had left to say.

"I don't think so," Kyle told him. "He says that Sam dying was just a bad turn and that he's sick of dealing with this whole affair."

"Is that so?"

"Yeah. He said he knows your claims are legal and that he wants to try and resolve the differences between you and him for good."

"Am I supposed to believe he won't just try and shoot me?"

A laugh gurgled at the back of Kyle's throat, but it wasn't out of anything he found humorous. Instead, it was more of an ironic laugh, which died almost as quickly as it had come. "He told me you were going to say that, and he said that if he wanted to kill you, he would have done it already."

As soon as Kyle said that, he averted his gaze even more. When Paul reached up to scratch his chin in contemplation, Kyle flinched as though a fist was headed his way.

"Adams is a smart man," Paul said to himself more than to anyone else in the room. "I heard that about him." Something else he'd heard was that Clint was more than good enough to make good on the claim that Kyle had just been talking about. Of course, that wasn't the sort of thing Paul was likely to admit in the presence of his own men.

"So when does he want to meet?" Paul asked casually.

"Tomorrow morning at the racetrack."

Castiglione nodded and pretended as though he actually needed to think it over. "Sounds good to me. Run back over to his hotel and leave a message. Tell him that I'll be more than happy to have a word with him."

Considering that the meeting was to be on his own turf after giving him plenty of time to prepare, Paul's statement was as genuine as the bloodthirsty grin on his face.

THIRTY-NINE

Cali Downs didn't run races every day of the year. In fact, it was closed more often than it was open and that was one of the biggest things that its newest owner wanted to change. Although not known throughout the entire country, Cali Downs was known well enough by folks within Texas and a few adjoining states. Even people from south of the border came to see the races, making those times when bets were being taken very profitable ones.

Word about the racetrack was going to spread. That was another thing that Paul Castiglione meant to do. And if that word came from the races themselves or the death of the famous Gunsmith, it didn't matter much to him. At the moment, the latter of those two was looking very appealing indeed.

Paul Castiglione stood outside of the smallest building within the track's property line. It was a building meant specifically for him and was off limits to the public in general. He intended on making an exception in Clint Adams's case, however, but that was mainly because he had more guns pointed at that building now than most forts had when the Indians were on the loose.

When he'd first opened the track for the day, Paul had

been in a downright chipper mood. A smile was on his face and steam was in his stride. Those two things lasted for a few hours before they finally started to fade.

Clint Adams hadn't shown after nearly a quarter of the day's races had been run. In that amount of time, Paul's mood had gone from chipper to sour. From there, it was only bound to get worse.

"You want me to go fetch him?" Bull asked hopefully.

Paul shook his head. "No need. I'm sure he'll show."

The big gunman grinned lecherously. "I'll bet he's fuckin' that blonde he brought with him from Labyrinth."

The thought of that brought Castiglione's mood down from annoyed to angry. "He'll be here," he growled. "He just wants to make me stew for a while, is all. I thought he'd be above that sort of thing."

"Maybe he left town," Kyle offered.

Bull looked over to the other man. While Kyle was almost as tall and had almost as much meat on his bones as Bull, his weight was mostly fat while Bull's was all muscle. It didn't take long for Bull's glare to back Kyle down.

"Yeah," the bigger gunman said. "You'd be real happy about that, wouldn't you?"

Paul didn't have to try too hard to block out the bickering around him. His eyes and ears were focused on the track in general, searching for any sign of Adams's arrival. As he looked around, he picked out the spots where the rest of his gunmen were posted. Each of them was in place and each of them was just as anxious for Clint Adams to show his face.

Locals and strangers alike wandered between the seats around the track and the betting windows. To them, this was just another day of spectacle and gambling. Only a few of them took pause from the intense looks on some of the armed men they passed. Even fewer of them actually recognized the face of the man walking past the betting windows with a pretty blonde hanging on to his arm.

"There he is," Paul said as a vicious smile replaced the angry scowl that he had been wearing.

Bull and Kyle turned to look in the direction that their boss was staring. Even the armed men posted around the track as lookouts weren't able to spot Clint before Castiglione had picked him out.

"Sure enough," Bull said. "And he's got that bitch with him."

"Shut your mouth, Bull," Paul ordered as he straightened up and prepared to greet Clint. "Don't even make a move unless I tell you or Adams goes for his gun."

Bull nodded, knowing damn well that if Clint Adams went for his gun, there probably wasn't a thing he could do about it until the Gunsmith's trigger had already been pulled. Of course, that wasn't the type of thing a gunman said to the man who was paying him.

Each of the gunmen as well as Paul Castiglione himself had plenty to think about when they saw Clint Adams walking toward them. For some, they wondered if this might be the day that changed the rest of their lives. Others wondered if this would be the last day of their lives. Whichever side of the fence they fell on, they were glad when Clint finally came to a stop a few paces in front of Castiglione.

"Morning, Paul," Clint said in a bright, somewhat cheery voice.

"Afternoon is more like it," Castiglione replied. "You took your own sweet time in getting here."

"I didn't know you'd be in such a hurry."

Clint knew exactly what he was doing. Despite the fact that he'd gotten up at the crack of dawn, he put off showing himself at the racetrack until just the right moment. Part of that was to show that he was still partially in control and another was just to let Paul stew in his own juices for a while.

Besides, it served Clint and Maggie well to have a big, leisurely breakfast.

"You killed one of my men," Paul said.

"Then why don't you go get the sheriff?" Clint asked, cutting right to the heart of things. "I'll wait right here." Pausing, Clint held Paul's gaze and cocked his head to one side. "I guess you'd know better than to do that, since you had every intention of your men bushwhacking me and killing me while my eyes were closed. That was the general idea, wasn't it?"

Paul winced as Clint's words cut right to the quick. He couldn't, however, refute them in the least. "I heard you wanted to meet with me, Adams. Here I am. There you are. Let's hear what you've got to say."

"All right then. I want those contracts you stole from Loren Janes."

"Stole? I don't know what you mean."

"Don't play around," Clint said. "We're way past that. I know about all the contracts you got, just like I know that any man with half a brain in his skull wouldn't have just handed them over to a man like you."

"I'm a businessman, Adams," Paul said, extending his arms as though he meant to embrace Clint in friendship. "I acquired them in a businesslike way."

"If you had enough money to buy those documents, you wouldn't be extorting from saloons and general stores."

Paul lowered his arms until one hand brushed against the holster buckled around his waist. That hand twitched slightly, but his impulse was tempered when he saw that Clint was watching every one of his moves the way a hawk eyed a mouse at the bottom of a canyon.

"Whether you pried those documents from Janes's dead hands or won them in a card game doesn't matter anymore," Clint said. "All that does matter is that you've got them and you're making too many people's lives difficult because of it."

"And I suppose you mean to do something about that?"

"If I didn't before, I sure as hell mean to now that you've tried to have me killed."

"Well, I ain't giving them up, Adams. Not to you or to anyone else. They're worth too much to me."

"You already got this place," Clint pointed out. "Wasn't that the whole idea?"

The surprise on Paul's face was plain to see. But, like a glimpse of the sun through a hole in the clouds, that peek behind the curtain was soon a memory. Rather than try to deny what Clint apparently already knew, Paul nodded. "Yeah," he said, "that was the idea at first. But there's more money to be had. Soon, I'll be able to build this place up even more and even build my own racetrack from the ground up. Add a couple of saloons and poker halls into the mix and I got myself a nice little empire. Now why would I want to go and hand all that over to you?"

"Because none of it was yours to begin with. You just picked up what a dead man dropped. Everything else after that doesn't matter one bit. You need to answer for the life of Loren Janes as well as all the money you stole from folks who were just trying to run their own lives."

"And how will you do that, Adams?" Paul asked. "By killing me? You harm one hair on my head and I guarantee you won't be any closer to them contracts."

"Oh, I have no doubt that you've paid that lawyer of yours well enough to see to that," Clint said.

Paul's eyes narrowed. While he'd been sure enough of himself so far, that confidence was beginning to fade into uncertainty. "What, then?"

"I'm proposing something that should be just your game. It's quick, easy, and will decide things once and for all."

"Really?"

"Sure. I do have other things I'd rather be doing than watching you and these trained monkeys of yours."

Castiglione smirked while the gunmen around him all gritted their teeth. "I'm still listening."

Clint motioned toward the open land behind him. "Let's race for it."

FORTY

"Did I hear you right?" Paul asked after taking a few moments to try and let Clint's words sink in. "You want to race?"

Clint nodded. "I know you've been keeping an eye on me. I'll wager you've done some checking on me since you first saw I was in Labyrinth."

Paul didn't say one word to confirm or deny that.

"Then I'll bet," Clint continued, "that you've also gotten a look at that stallion of mine that brought me here."

"The Darley Arabian?" Paul asked, unable to hide the admiration in his eyes.

"That's the one," Clint confirmed with a nod.

Zack had been so quiet during this exchange that it was more than easy to overlook him entirely. That, added to the fact that he was the sort of diminutive little squirt who blended into the background anyway, made him practically invisible.

At this, though, he broke away from the corner where he had been quietly sitting and stepped up close to Paul's side and started nudging his elbow, all the while, trying his level best to fix a threatening stare upon Clint.

To Clint's credit, he somehow managed to keep from laughing in the little guy's face.

"You can't be seriously thinking about this, Paul," Zack whispered. "I've seen that horse and it's—"

"Shut up," Paul interrupted.

"Besides the horse, how do we know that Adams won't try anything funny? I mean, he's probably been riding that horse for years. I've seen horses like that in the circus. They can pull tricks you ain't never even seen before."

Although he seemed lost in his own thoughts, Paul did take heed of what the smaller fellow was saying. "I may not be the smartest fella in the world, but I know better than to bite on the first deal that comes along."

"I don't know what you've heard about me, but I'm not a cheat," Clint said.

"And you ain't no jockey, either. Why would you want to do something like this?"

Shrugging, Clint said, "All right then. How about we play cards for those contracts? Do you know how to play poker?"

Paul's head started shaking so quickly that he looked like he might be having a fit. His hand came up as well to waggle a finger in Clint's direction. "Oh, no. I ain't playing cards with you for them kind of stakes."

Apparently, the stories circulating about Clint didn't all have to do with his speed with a gun.

"Then I guess you're stuck with me," Clint said.

"Or I could just say no to this whole deal. After all, it's not like you've got me pressed up against the wall on this."

"That's true." Lowering his voice just enough to let Paul know how serious he was, Clint added, "But if we go through with this, I'm out of the picture one way or another. Win or lose, you won't have to worry about me poking around in your affairs any longer. If you do see my face again, it'll be just two fellas passing each other on the street."

Paul's eyes narrowed a bit as he thought that over. The simple fact that he was still considering it proved that he'd heard about some other instances where Clint had followed through on someone else all the way to the end.

After letting a bit of time pass in silence, Clint shrugged and started to turn away. "Doesn't matter to me. I've got nothing else better to do, and I never mind going out of my way for a friend. Seems like I'd do more good here than the law and I know for damn sure that I don't have to worry about any of these so-called gunmen of yours."

That caused Bull to bristle, but with Sam dead and Kyle battered and bruised, there wasn't much sense in arguing Clint's statement.

"All right then," Clint said with a backhanded wave. "I guess I'll be going. I've got another hunch on some horses to bet while I'm here."

"Hold it," Paul said grudgingly, yet insistently. When he saw Clint turn back around to look at him, Castiglione let out a breath. "Whichever way it turns out, I'm done with you after your horse runs in this race?"

Clint nodded. "I win and I get those documents. All of those documents."

"And if you lose?"

"Then I walk out of town and leave you to your business. If my friend asks me to step in on his behalf in this matter, I'll pass and tell him I already did my best."

"That's not enough."

"No?"

"I want my money back," Paul grunted. "That money you won from me the other day. If you lose, I want that money back. Every cent of it."

After taking a moment for himself, Clint nodded. "Fair enough. So who rides my horse?"

"I've got plenty of jockeys working for me. You can pick any of them you like."

Narrowing his eyes and smirking humorlessly, Clint

said, "Come on now. Do you think I'm stupid? I'd just as soon let the girl ride that horse than of anyone on your payroll."

Castiglione smirked lecherously. "I'll agree to that."

"You'll agree to what?" Clint asked.

"You want her to ride? I can abide by that."

Clint rolled his eyes before glancing over at Maggie. She looked back at him with a not-too-subtle shake of her head. Despite her silent refusal, Clint nodded. "Fine. It's a deal."

Paul smiled like he'd already won the race. "We'll settle this tonight. One hour after the last scheduled race."

Clint was already walking away, practically dragging Maggie behind him. "Fine, fine," he muttered.

"And no more bets!" Paul shouted at their backs.

FORTY-ONE

Clint and Maggie walked in a huff from the racetrack. They went right past the betting widows without so much as a sideways glance. They even walked past the gunmen posted nearby, which had been easier for Clint to spot than a black feather on a white duck's back.

Neither of them said a word to each other until Cali Downs was behind them and they were standing on a corner a few streets away. Only then did Maggie allow herself to look over at Clint and study the blank expression on his face.

"Do you think I overdid it?" she asked.

Clint didn't want to smirk, but he was unable to hold it back any longer. "You did great. For a moment, even I was thinking that you didn't want to ride Eclipse in that race."

Sensing that it was all right for her to show her own emotions, Maggie jumped a little in place before composing herself once again. "That was beautiful, Clint! How did you know he'd go for the race?"

"He's a gambler. Besides, with the offer I gave him there wasn't much of a way for him to refuse. To be honest, I thought he'd ask for more money if he lost."

Maggie shook her head in admiration. "What amazes

me even more is that you got it so I would ride Eclipse at all. I thought for certain he would recognize me from working at the stables in Labyrinth."

"If you don't personally owe him money, I doubt he even bothers knowing you exist. Besides, he's the sort of man who tends to overlook women who aren't bringing him food or warming his bed. Speaking of which . . ."

Maggie gave Clint a playful smack on the arm. "Clint Adams! You think you can just order me into bed whenever you get the urge?"

"Actually, I was thinking more along the lines of getting something to eat."

Maggie winked at him and said, "And I was just kidding about refusing that first offer. Looks like Paul's not the only one who doesn't know when to push a deal just a little further."

Shaking his head, Clint offered Maggie his arm and led her to the closest restaurant. They both walked with a spring in their steps and smiles on their faces.

"We did a good job here," Clint said before their celebratory mood got the better of them. "But that doesn't mean it's all downhill from here. Paul's also the type of man to protect his investments, and this race is one hell of an investment."

"I'll win it," Maggie said with utter confidence. "Don't you worry about that. Besides, I think Eclipse is aching to tear up some ground even if his feet were stuck halfway in the mud. Paul couldn't have anything to compare to that in his stables."

"That's not what I meant." Clint stopped and turned so that he was looking straight into Maggie's eyes. "Castiglione cheated and killed to get where he is today. I doubt he'll stop now."

"You think he might try something during the race?"

"I don't think. I know he will. The question is if you still want to take that risk."

Maggie pulled in a breath and returned Clint's gaze. "Will you be there to help in case things get too bad?" she asked.

"I'll be there to make sure they don't get that far. That doesn't mean that Paul or one of his boys won't get lucky. Whatever happens or whatever he's got in store, I'll be there to cover you."

"Then I'll ride in that race."

"Are you sure?"

"I trust you, Clint. Besides, if I can't count on the Gunsmith to cover me, then who on earth could I count on?"

Clint studied her face carefully. If he saw even the slightest bit of hesitancy, he intended on coming up with something else. But Maggie's eyes were sure, her hands were steady, and there was nothing else he could read between the lines of what she was saying.

"All right then," he said. "Looks like we're still on for a race."

"What about the rest of what he had planned? We've still got some time to kill."

"Wouldn't you like to take Eclipse out for a bit to get a feel for him?"

"That won't take but a few minutes. I was the one who exercised him while you were away, after all."

"Yeah, but you know as well as I do that going out for a ride is a whole lot different than running at full gallop."

Clint recognized the guilty way that Maggie turned her face away from him.

"Wait a second," Clint said. "You did just exercise him, right?"

She shrugged and flashed Clint a guilty smile. "Eclipse is a fine horse. I've only seen one come along that nice once or twice in the years I've been working with them. Besides, he was aching to get out and run."

Clint rolled his eyes. "Now I know why I get such a good rate at those stables of yours. Glad you enjoyed yourself."

"If I hadn't, then I wouldn't be so certain of riding this race. Tell you the truth, I think I'm just as excited to be going that fast around that track as Eclipse will be."

"If you're certain, then that's the important thing. Let's get something to eat."

Maggie didn't budge when Clint started walking. Instead, she looked at him in a way that said she was thinking more along the lines of the second option they'd been discussing. The hunger in her eyes had nothing at all to do with food.

"I can't believe I'm going to say this, but we should save that for later," Clint told her, albeit grudgingly. "You need to be at your best for the race."

"Fine," Maggie pouted. "I guess it's just something to eat then. But I expect some royal treatment after I win."

"Don't worry," Clint said while wrapping one arm around her shapely waist. "You'll get it."

FORTY-TWO

The last race had been run and there were only a few stragglers lazing about the betting windows as well as the track itself. Those stragglers were of the two-legged variety and most of them seemed to be griping to each other about the money they'd lost or the horses that seemed to have lost their will to run at the worst possible moment.

The winners were mostly to be found at the saloons, bragging about their foresight and tossing around betting tips as though luck had nothing at all to do with their profits.

Apart from those few stragglers, the only other people still to be seen at Cali Downs were either Paul Castiglione or on his payroll. With a signal from Paul, Bull made the rounds to see that all those stragglers quickly found their way off the track. Once the place was cleared out, Bull came back to where Paul was standing and gave him a nod.

"That's the last of 'em," Bull grunted.

Although Paul nodded, he didn't look all that happy about it. "Good. Make certain there ain't nobody else around."

"Already did. I checked twice."

Paul's eyes glinted over to the big gunman, but he nodded one more time before saying anything. "All right."

"You expect Adams will show?"

"If he doesn't, I guess we might as well come after him with everything we got. From what I heard, that'd be a whole lot easier than trying to take him on."

"I bet half the things we heard about him ain't nothing but saloon talk."

Paul let out a single, burp of a laugh. "Even so, would you want to take your chances against him?"

"I would."

"Yeah, well I know plenty of others that thought the same thing. They're either dead, in jail, or they got themselves set so far back that those first two don't look so bad. Adams is like a dog with his teeth sunk into a bone. Once it gets past a certain point, there's gonna be blood spilled."

Bull nodded and grunted under his breath. It wasn't in his nature to give another man such a big benefit of the doubt. Then again, when that man was the Gunsmith, he didn't have too many other choices.

"Still," Paul added with a wry grin, "there's not much reason for us to be too upset about this deal. Since it was his suggestion, Adams is going to show. He's not the sort to run and even if he was, we'd pick him off before he crossed town limits."

"We sure would," Bull replied. "I put that rifleman on top of the feed store just like you asked. He can see nearly every street from there."

"But he's not going to run. He ain't going to win, either. If Adams was riding that horse of his himself, he might have a shot. But with that bitch in the saddle against my best jockey on top of my best horse, there ain't a prayer that he's coming out on top of this deal."

Bull was shifting on his feet and finally got himself to speak his mind. "She might have a shot. I think I recognize her from Labyrinth. I've seen her riding some wild broncos once or twice."

"That doesn't matter," Paul replied, waving off the comment as though it were just a fly buzzing around his nose. "Even if she's the best rider in the country, she can't ride with a bullet in her. And there ain't a horse alive who can win a race once he's been shot. Of course, that's a last resort, right?"

Bull nodded. "That's right. Them's were the orders I got from you and them's were the same orders I passed along."

"How many guns have you got posted around here?"

Pointing toward the rows of seats, Bull said, "There's one over there looking out at one end of the track. There's one in the stables looking out at the other end of the track and there's another up over there," he added, nodding toward the building where the bets were taken. "He can see damn near everything from up there."

Paul smiled a little wider as he glanced around at the spots Bull had pointed out. The expression on his face when he was done resembled that of an emperor surveying his lands.

"Should we kill Adams if we get a clear shot?" Bull asked.

"Not unless he makes a move first. Humbling the Gunsmith could be just as good as killing him. Either way, once the word gets out, we become so famous that nobody in the country will think about crossing us again. But don't do a damn thing until I get my money back. After that, if an opportunity presents itself, there's no reason to pass it up."

Bull nodded slowly. His eyes were already partly glazed over and his mouth was open in a cruel smile.

Although they were showing it differently, both men were thinking the same thing.

This was going to be one hell of a night.

FORTY-THREE

The sun sat low on the western horizon when Clint led Eclipse onto the tack at Cali Downs. Maggie sat in the Darley Arabian's saddle, doing a fairly good job of looking hesitant about the ride to come. Clint's eyes were focused on the men scattered around the track. What bothered him more than the gunmen he did see were the ones he didn't. By his count, there were at least three unaccounted for.

"I knew you'd show up," Paul said as he strutted forward.

Clint came to a stop close to the track, but several paces away from Castiglione. "Why wouldn't I?"

"Some of my men thought you might have reconsidered this whole race idea. It's not too late for that, you know. Reconsider, that is."

"Nah. I think I'll go through with it. Besides, we're all here and Eclipse is ready to go."

"Fine. Then you shouldn't mind upping the stakes."

"What did you have in mind?"

"I win and you double the money you won from me. Plus, you'll owe me a favor that I can call in anytime I please."

"And what if I win?" Clint asked.

"Then I'll not only hand over those contracts, but I'll pay back all I took from the folks in Labyrinth."

Clint knew damn well that there were plenty of other folks in plenty of other towns who deserved to get back what was coming to them. But since that money was already gone, Clint figured he was doing plenty by putting a stop to Castiglione's demands.

"You got yourself a deal," Clint said.

"Good." When Paul stepped forward with his hand extended, he revealed a slender figure who'd been standing behind him and Bull. "And just to make sure everything's square, I brought along a witness to the deal."

The moment Clint spotted Harold Meyer's face, he was surprised. A moment after that, he realized that he should have expected as much. "You carry that lawyer with you wherever you go?" Clint asked.

"Every now and then he does come in handy. We still on?"

Clint grasped Paul's hand and shook it. "We're on." Shifting his eyes to Meyer, Clint added, "Just so long as he keeps you in line as well."

Meyer lifted his chin proudly. "I'm here as impartial counsel and witness only. My prior dealings with Mister Castiglione will have no bearing on this transaction."

"Good," Clint said. "Then let's get this over with."

Eclipse and Paul's horse were the only two on the track. Blue Beetle was a lithe gelding with a coat so shiny that it was what undoubtedly earned him his name. The fading light from the sky glistened off his coat, making it look like blue, oiled steel. Eclipse walked up to the starting line and glanced over to his competition as if he wasn't impressed.

"That's it, boy," Maggie said as she reached out to pat the stallion's neck. "You let him know who's boss."

The jockey on Blue Beetle's back was a skinny man in his early twenties. Although his arms were covered with a layer of tight muscle, he still looked as though a stiff wind could blow him across the Mexican border. He looked over to Maggie and gave her a cocky smile.

"You do much riding?" he asked.

"Some."

"Ever ridden in a race?"

"No," Maggie replied honestly. "Not an official one."

"It's a whole new world, lady. Riding to the farm and back is one thing, riding the whirlwind is another. That's what a race is like. It's like sitting on top of a twister and hanging on for your life. You think you can do that?"

"I shouldn't fall from the saddle, if that's what you mean."

The smile on his face got a little cockier. "Oh, I wouldn't be so sure about that."

The seats were empty except for Paul and Bull perched on the edge of the bottommost bench. Paul looked around idly at first, but with growing impatience.

"Where's Adams?" Paul asked.

Bull grunted before replying. "He and that lawyer went off to talk somewhere."

"Fine," Paul said with a grin. "Adams can talk till he's blue in the face and he won't get Meyer to budge. Screw 'em both. Let's get this over with."

Saying that, Paul stood up and drew his pistol. "Ready! GO!"

FORTY-FOUR

Clint had been talking to Meyer, sure enough. At least, he'd found something to talk to the lawyer about, which was enough to get him away from the open and out of sight. Once he was inside the stables, Clint drew his gun and dropped his voice to a harsh whisper.

"This isn't about you, Meyer, so don't panic."

Meyer's eyes widened into saucers, and he would have let out a yelp if he'd been able to pull in enough breath.

"See that rope over there?" Clint asked, nodding toward a length coiled around a hook nearby. "Get it and then walk over to that corner."

"Wh-what are you g-going to d-do?" Meyer stammered.

"I just need to get you out of the way and make sure you stay there."

"I won't move. I s-swear it."

"Yeah, well forgive me if I'm not inclined to believe you. Working for Castiglione and being a lawyer are two misfortunes that I just can't overlook. Now get over there, sit down, and hold your hands out past that post."

Meyer was standing in a dark corner. He squatted down until he dropped onto his backside and then held out both arms so that they were on either side of a post with his wrists extending past it.

"You done this before?" Clint asked lightheartedly while tying Meyer's hands together. "Now open wide."

The lawyer was confused, but followed Clint's pantomimed lead and opened his mouth as widely as he could. He recoiled a bit, but didn't resist when Clint stuffed a bandanna into his mouth.

"Can you breathe all right?" Clint asked.

Meyer nodded.

"Good. Now sit tight and keep quiet. Believe me, when you hear the hell that's about to break loose, you'll thank me for stowing you away in here."

Meyer pulled in a few breaths that sounded like labored wheezing even though they were just being sucked in through his nose. His heart was beating so fast that he thought it might pound its way out through his chest. When he screwed up enough courage to look back in Clint's direction, he couldn't even see the first trace of the man.

The lawyer might as well have been tied up by a ghost.

Clint was just about to leave the stables when he stopped in mid-stride. Meyer had been too busy trying not to soil himself and it had seemed like the perfect time to take his leave.

There were gunmen missing and a race happening with a lot of Paul Castiglione's money at stake. In Clint's mind, that meant those gunmen were probably scattered around somewhere waiting to get the jump on Clint or Maggie. The race itself was most likely fixed. Otherwise, Paul would never had agreed to it.

Having put his trust in Maggie and gone over some things for her to watch for, Clint's only course of action was to make sure the rest of the track was clear. On the way over, he'd scoured the buildings overlooking Cali Downs that were within rifle range. If there were snipers, they would have to be at the track itself.

That was why, when he heard something moving in the loft over his head, Clint froze in his tracks.

He'd already holstered the Colt, so his hand lowered toward the pistol as he turned. Before Clint could even get around to get a look at where the noise had come from, he heard the rustling overhead become a fast-paced thumping. Whoever was up there was now racing to get a better angle before Clint could do the same.

Outside, the sound of Paul's voice was carried through the air. That was followed by the crack of his pistol, marking the start of the race.

Maggie snapped Eclipse's reins and touched her heels to the Darley Arabian's sides. Those things, combined with the sound of the gun, were more than enough to make the stallion explode forward like he was running from a burning barn.

Next to her, Blue Beetle's jockey had taken a split-second head start. Although that was illegal, she knew better than to think it would be counted against him. Maggie wasn't too worried about that since Eclipse had already rushed up and closed the gap between himself and the other horse.

Just as she was going to pull ahead slightly, Maggie felt something smack against her forehead. For a moment, she thought a bug might have gotten in her way, but the stinging was too much for it to have been caused by an unlucky insect.

All she needed to do was look to her right to see the jockey on Blue Beetle cocking his arm back to hit her a second time with the crop in his hand. Maggie ducked at just the right moment to let the crop hiss over her head. From there, she needed to look at where she was going. Even if she was inclined to hit the jockey back, she didn't have anything handy to do so.

Cracking the reins like a whip, she tightened her legs against Eclipse's sides. The Darley Arabian shook his head in protest to the sting of leather, but charged forward like a runaway train.

They were approaching a turn and Blue Beetle was getting much too close for comfort.

As Maggie leaned into the turn, she felt her own body conforming to the powerful motions of the horse beneath her. The next thing she felt was the crack of a crop against her back followed by the push of heaving ribs against her leg.

Blue Beetle was pressing against her in an effort to force Eclipse into the inside rail. Timing it perfectly between strides, Maggie plucked her leg out from between the two animals and delivered a sideways kick into the other jockey's side.

It wasn't enough to clear Blue Beetle's saddle, but it sure gave her a little more breathing room.

FORTY-FIVE

A rifle shot punched through the loft over Clint's head. He'd been running for cover beneath the same wooden platform where the rifleman himself was standing. At the first trace of the gunshot, Clint launched himself forward using both legs and aimed for a nearby bale of hay.

The bullet knocked a hole through the loft over Clint's head and tore through an adjacent bale of hay. Clint's hands brushed against the floor with the rest of his body following soon after. As he was tucking into a forward roll that would take him even farther beneath the loft, another shot from the rifle broke through the wooden barrier.

Lead whipped through the air, working its way closer and closer to Clint. Stopping himself with a quickly outstretched foot, Clint landed with his back against the floor. His eyes traced the holes above him in a split second. After that, he caught the glimmer of movement through one of the freshly made holes.

What followed after that was mostly reflex.

The instant Clint saw the slightest trace of the rifleman through a hole, he plucked the Colt from its holster and aimed in one fluid motion. He pulled the trigger six times with a heartbeat in between each shot.

180

Six more holes were drilled up through the loft, placed in a pattern that was meant to cover the area where the rifleman had to be. Two of those shots caught nothing but wood and air. One of those shots clipped a bit of flesh and blood. The remaining three knocked the rifleman off his feet and toward the edge of the loft.

Clint had removed the spent shells and was replacing them with fresh ones from his gun belt when he heard another series of movements. The Colt's cylinder snapped shut, but wasn't needed just then. The only motion that was left for Clint to see was the rifleman's body falling from the loft to land less than ten feet away from him.

Getting to his feet, Clint checked over the stables before rushing out. He'd already picked out several potential spots for more attackers and was on his way to the next one as Meyer looked on from his spot. The lawyer had no intention of trying to get away. In fact, he even scooted as far into the shadows as his bonds would allow.

Paul stomped his feet and pumped his hands in the air. He could hear rifle shots in the distance, which brought a wicked smile to his face. "About damn time," he grunted. Now he just waited to see how long that blond bitch could stay in the saddle.

He and Bull had a side bet going. As long as his boys shot the rider instead of the horse, Paul won even more money. Castiglione got to his feet and cheered for Blue Beetle while inside he was cheering for a headshot from one of his boys.

"There you go, bitch," Zack whispered as he pressed his cheek against the stock of his rifle. "Just round that bend and stick your neck out for me."

The short fellow was stretched out on top of the building where the betting windows were located. His legs were splayed out behind him for balance and the barrel of his rifle was just barely poking out over the edge of the roof.

His finger tightened around his trigger as he pulled in a slow, steadying breath. When he let that breath out, his finger would squeeze the trigger and he would put a round through Maggie's skull as if it were a melon sitting on a fencepost.

He held his breath for a moment. He started to let it out.

"Hello there, Zack," came a vaguely familiar voice from not too far away.

Zack glanced over to find a familiar, if unwelcome, figure crouched at a spot not too far from the top of the ladder used to reach the roof. Even though he recognized Clint's face, Zack still had a hard time believing what he was seeing.

The small fellow decided his fate in a heartbeat. In a quick burst of motion, he swung his rifle around and prepared to fire.

A shot did sound through the air, but it came from Clint's Colt. He'd drawn the modified pistol so quickly that Zack hadn't even seen a hint of it.

The Colt's shot caught Zack in the forehead, snapped his head back, and exploded out the other side in a mess of brains and blood.

Clint walked over to the twitching body and bent down to scoop up the rifle. "Good-bye Zack," he said.

Maggie heard the shots being fired, but only because she'd been waiting for them. Although Blue Beetle's jockey was still trying to hit her with his crop, push Eclipse into the rail, or even shove her out of the saddle, he wasn't having much success. After all, it was hard to do much to a target that was consistently out of reach.

Eclipse was single-minded in his purpose. His hooves pounded against the track and his head churned back and forth like a steam-driven piston. Froth formed at the corners of his mouth and a lather was beginning to issue from his coat, but most of that came from pure excitement.

Never in his life had he been allowed to run full-out under such conditions. The more Blue Beetle tried to pass him, the faster Eclipse wanted to go.

The more the other jockey tried to cheat, the more Maggie wanted to see him fail.

In the end, there was too much for Blue Beetle to overcome, and Eclipse thundered across the finish line several lengths ahead of his competition.

Just when she was thinking her victory had been easy, Maggie saw Paul and Bull storming out to greet them. Needless to say, they weren't happy for her.

FORTY-SIX

"What in the hell is going on here?" Paul fumed. "What the hell do I pay you men for? Kyle," he said over his shoulder, "blow this bitch's head off."

The portly gunman stepped out from where he'd been hiding behind the second set of seats across from the betting windows. A rifle shot cracked through the air, but it didn't come from Kyle's gun.

Looking down at the wound that had seemed to magically appear in his shoulder, Kyle brought his gun up again and sighted down the barrel at Maggie.

Another shot came. This time, it obviously came from the area of the betting windows. Unfortunately, this discovery came too late for Kyle since he was already finding it difficult to breathe. It was just as difficult to stand up. He felt light-headed as he started to drop. The bullet had passed so cleanly through his heart that he didn't even know he was dying until the Reaper had already claimed him.

Paul looked back and forth so quickly that he nearly cracked his neck. "What in the . . . ?"

Then he saw Clint step away from the nearby building with rifle in hand. A few steps more, and Clint pitched the rifle away so he could free up his hand to hang down next to his holstered Colt.

Maggie was patting Eclipse on the head while talking to him in a soothing tone. Slowly, but surely, her voice was calming the Darley Arabian down. She rode toward Clint, but kept her distance when she saw him signal to her.

Paul squared his shoulders, feeling confident since he had one gunman to his left and Bull to his right. "Five hundred dollars goes to the man that kills Adams."

Clint shook his head slowly. "Just hand over the documents, Paul. You don't want to do this."

"The hell I don't. Five hundred. Who's gonna take it?"

The gunman next to Paul licked his lips nervously and ignored the warning glare Clint gave him. One moment the younger man was drawing his pistol, and the next he was reeling back as Clint's bullet tore a cavern through his chest.

Slowly, Clint reholstered the Colt.

"Your lawyer's back there," Clint said. "He saw the whole thing. Just hold up your end and this will all be over."

Paul thought it over before grinning and leaning toward his right. "Bull, rip his head off and bring it to me."

Judging by the twitch in Bull's eye, there was nothing more that he'd rather do. But his anger was tempered by something else. Although he wasn't happy about it, Bull forced his head down, turned his back on Paul and started walking away from the racetrack altogether.

"There now," Clint said, genuinely surprised. "I guess even a bull's got a brain or two. What about you, Paul? Are you willing to do the right thing?"

Paul sputtered and tried to talk. He even tried to curse Clint's name, but all he managed to get out were a few incomprehensible grunts. He reached under his jacket, causing Clint's hand to flinch toward his gun. But instead of a pistol, Castiglione pulled a wad of folded papers from his pocket.

"Here." Paul grunted. "That's all of 'em." And then he tossed them onto the ground so they spilled out into a messy pile at Clint's feet.

Clint lowered himself to one knee and reached down to scoop the papers up. At that moment, he saw Paul take half a step back while making a clumsy reach for his gun. Giving him the last possible chance, Clint waited until Paul cleared leather before snatching the Colt from his own holster and taking aim.

Two shots cracked through the air.

Paul's hissed out into open space while Clint's buried itself deep into Castiglione's gut.

Shaking his head at the man's lethal stubbornness, Clint stood up again and flipped through the papers. Maggie rode Eclipse up beside him and swung down from the saddle.

"What about Bull?" she asked. "You think he'll come back?"

Clint shook his head. "He's got no reason to." He then singled out one paper in particular and looked it over.

"What's that?" Maggie asked.

"A document Rick will be very pleased to see. In fact," he added, folding the papers up and stuffing them into his pocket, "all of these papers need to go back to their rightful owners."

"Do you know for certain if Loren Janes is really dead? I mean, they are his documents after all."

"I'm not sure if he is or not. Either way, there's plenty of work that needs to be done to set all of this straight again. What I can tell you is that I'm sick to death of this whole thing. Come on," Clint said, draping one arm around Maggie and taking Eclipse's reins with the other. "I've got a lawyer on retainer for just such an occasion."

Watch for

SCORPION'S TALE

284th novel in the exciting GUNSMITH series
from Jove

Coming in August!

J. R. ROBERTS

THE GUNSMITH